Celebrating
THE
WORD

Celebrating THE WORD

EARL RADMACHER
AND THE STAFF AT WESTERN SEMINARY

MULTNOMAH · PRESS

Portland, Oregon 97266

Scripture versions quoted in this book include *The New American Standard Bible,* © The Lockman Foundation 1960, 1962, 1963, 1968, 1971, 1972, 1973, 1975, 1977, and used by permission; *The Holy Bible: New International Version,* copyright 1973, 1978, 1984 by the International Bible Society, and used by permission of Zondervan Bible Publishers; *The Holy Bible, New King James Version,* copyright © 1982 by Thomas Nelson, Inc.; and the King James Version.

Cover design by Bruce DeRoos

CELEBRATING THE WORD
© 1987 by Western Conservative Baptist Seminary
Published by Multnomah Press
Portland, Oregon 97266

Multnomah Press is a ministry of Multnomah School of the Bible, 8435 NE Glisan Street, Portland, Oregon 97220.

Printed in the United States of America

Library of Congress Cataloging-in-Publication Data

Celebrating the word.

   Twelve essays commemorating the 60th anniversary of
Western Seminary in Portland, Or.
   Includes bibliographies.
   1. Bible—Evidences, authority, etc. 2. Bible—
Inspiration. 3. Bible—Theology. 4. Word of God
(Theology) 5. Western Seminary (Portland, Or.)
I. Western Seminary (Portland, Or.)
BS480.C4   1987   220.1   87-14680
ISBN 0-88070-207-9 (pbk.)

87 88 89 90 91 92 92 – 10 9 8 7 6 5 4 3 2 1

CONTENTS

INTRODUCTION

W e are witnessing today a revival of interest in the Bible. Discernible in pew and pulpit alike, this recovery of focus on the Bible can be sensed in the expansion of Bible study groups within churches of virtually all denominations, and it is reflected in a fresh and strong emphasis upon authentic expository preaching. Thousands of believers are coming to church on Sunday morning demanding to be fed the unadulterated Word of God and they are expecting their preachers to be skilled interpreters and appliers of the Scriptures.

For too long the Bible had been strangely silent in many of our churches. To be sure, it had been appealed to as the only rule for faith and practice among most evangelical churches, and it remained the text source for most of the sermons. Yet, too often its use was focused on the promotion of only certain key doctrines or pet doctrinal emphases. Worse, it was preached and taught as mere doctrinal information to congregations who grew increasingly numb to its hearing.

It is not as though the church has been without the Bible. Indeed, there has never been a period in the history of the church when the Bible itself was so present and plentiful. A recent Christian periodical took note of that fact in calling attention to over 58 different English language versions of the Scriptures. It pointed out that at least 50 Bible publishers print over 2,670 different Bibles in at least 34 different translations. Most Christians in the United States own more than one translation—and yet it is this generation of the church that has been called a biblically illiterate generation.

Still, today there are vital signs of recovery, signs of hunger for the penetrating, life-changing relevance of the Bible. With this volume, twelve members of the faculty of Western Conservative Baptist Seminary in Portland, Oregon, raise the banner of the Bible aloft and call for a celebration—a celebration of the Word. Focusing on this lofty theme, each of the following chapters seeks to treat the Scriptures as a brilliance and beauty. In each case, the intention is also to demonstrate that special aspect of the Word in its relation to the very practical disciplines and functions of ministry. The authors of these chapters prepared and delivered them originally as messages in a conference on the Bible in the chapel of Western Seminary.

This book has another special and more personal meaning for the Western Seminary community. Nineteen eighty-seven marks a significant anniversary year—its sixtieth. On the chilly evening of 4 October 1927, Western Seminary was officially opened with a dedication service at the Hinson Memorial Baptist Church in Portland. The speaker was Dr. J. J. Ross, pastor of First Baptist Church of Vancouver, British Columbia. His subject: "The Inspiration of the Scriptures." It was a great address by a great man of God, and could scarcely have been better selected for the occasion. It marked out the footing upon which the school would be built, and if anything stands out most enduringly in the sixty-year history of Western Seminary, it is this demonstrated commitment to uphold and teach the Word of God with scholarly fidelity and personal warmth and passion.

This volume focuses on that commitment as we celebrate our sixtieth anniversary. Besides the diligent work of the twelve faculty members contributing, this volume has involved the input of several others who have sacrificially served to bring it to fruition: Mr. Mike Winter, vice president of development, who so ably served as Sixtieth Anniversary Chairman; Dr. Stanley A. Ellisen, who coordinated the chapel offerings and directed the compilation in book form; Mrs. Betty Lou Johnstone, Mrs. Ruth Ann Tidswell, and Miss Bonnie Ekholm, who helped with the copy editing; and Mrs. Ruth Wolf and Mrs. Charlotte Lawrence, who patiently typed and re-typed the manuscripts for publishing. We gratefully acknowledge the dedicated contribution of each of these who have helped make this volume possible. We would finally express our thanks to the editors of Multnomah Press who have encouraged the publication project and have put the final product in such an eminently attractive and readable form.

We offer this work then with the prayer that it might be a further contribution to the nurturing of the church as it feeds on the inerrant and eternal Word of God. It is our "Celebration of the Word."

> "Open my eyes that I may see
> wonderful things in Thy Law."   Psalm 119:19

> James E. Sweeney, Ph.D.
> Academic Vice President
> and Dean of the Faculty
> Western Baptist Seminary

Psalm 119:17-18 is a prayer that should be the petition of all who consider the various aspects of the Word of God: "Do good to your servant and I will live. I will obey your word, open my eyes that I may see wonderful things in your Law."

It is fitting that this celebration of the Bible should be inaugurated by **Dr. Earl Radmacher.** *Not only has he been Western Seminary's president since 1965, he is truly a man of the Word. He has given his life and ministry uncompromisingly to the study, defense, and exposition of Scripture. Here he establishes the groundwork for all of the subsequent chapters by centering our minds upon the authority and the truth of God's Word.*

C H A P T E R 1

THE WORD AS TRUTH:
Its Authority

EARL D. RADMACHER

GOD Almighty is ultimate authority. From Jesus' prayer in John 17 we learn that God has given all authority to Jesus Christ (17:2) and that Jesus has communicated that authority to us in the Word—which Word, Jesus says, is truth (17:17).

This prayer in John 17—which Jesus prayed after His last discourse with His disciples and just before He made His way across the Kidron Valley to the Garden of Gethsemane—may truly be called the Lord's Prayer. Let us move back to see what preceded it and how Jesus used the Word—the Word which He believed to have full authority.

JESUS DEMONSTRATING THE TRUTH

Jesus, the Master Teacher, did not get locked into one methodology as many of us do. In fact, one doctoral study revealed that Jesus changed His teaching methodology in the gospel of John more than a hundred times.

In John 13, we see several examples of the way Jesus used the Word, beginning with the demonstration by modeling.

Notice His mindset in verse three:

> Jesus, *knowing* [italics mine] that the Father had given
> all things into His hands, and that He had come from
> God and was going to God . . .

John tells us the source of Jesus' actions. They grew out
of the truth He knew. He could do what He did because He
knew what He knew. He knew from where He came; He knew
where He was going; He knew His mission. He knew all these
truths on the basis of the authoritative Word of God, and the
knowledge of them set Him free to do what He did in taking
the role of a servant.

This is precisely the pattern Jesus gave to those who
would desire to be His disciples.

> If you abide in My word, you are My disciples indeed.
> And you shall know the truth and the truth shall make
> you free. (John 8:31b-32)

Before John records the action of Christ, he therefore
gives us the source of the action. This principle is absolutely
basic to Christlike action.[1]

David put it succinctly: "Thy word have I hidden in my
heart in order that I may not sin against Thee" (Psalm 119:11).

With this clue as to why Jesus was able to do what He
did, the biographer goes on to recount Christ's demonstration
of servant-leadership as He washes the disciples' feet (13:4-11).

It is not my purpose to make a detailed analysis of this
action that is so familiar to us. Jesus, knowing what He knew
(13:1-3), "rose from supper, and laid aside His garments, took
a towel and girded Himself. After that He poured water into
a basin and began to wash the disciples' feet."

Here was a need that no one else had met. If this had
been Jesus' own home, a servant boy likely would have done
this very ordinary duty of washing the guests' feet. The disciples
obviously were not up to doing such a menial endeavor, or
else they would have done it before their teacher did. But why

were they intimidated by such a task? Why so restrained and insecure?

They really didn't know who they were. And they didn't know who they were because they really didn't know who Christ was, as was revealed later:

> And suddenly, one of those who were with Jesus stretched out his hand and drew his sword, struck the servant of the high priest, and cut off his ear. Then Jesus said to him, "Put your sword in its place, for all who take the sword will perish by the sword. Or do you think that I cannot now pray to My Father, and He will provide Me with more than twelve legions of angels?" (Matthew 26:51-53)

And they didn't know who He was because they really didn't know who God was. They measured themselves by each other. Comparing himself to Andrew, Peter saw himself as greater. *So,* Peter felt for sure, *if anyone ought to wash their feet, it certainly shouldn't be me; it ought to be Andrew.* James and John, the Sons of Thunder, certainly were not considering washing one another's feet or anyone else's. Simon the Zealot, the right-winger, was certainly not considering washing the feet of Matthew the Publican, the left-winger.

This group had all the seeds of dissension. It was a good cross-section of humanity, typical of any group of immature believers. None was ready to be a servant.

But Jesus was—for He knew who He was. He knew where He came from. He knew where He was going. And knowing all of that, He took off His outer garment, stripped down to the garb of a servant, and began to wash their feet. Knowing what He knew, He was secure. Taking the role of a servant did not intimidate Him.

If the disciples had problems before, they had greater problems now. Though they weren't about to wash each other's feet, they had enough sense to understand that it certainly wasn't Jesus' role to do it. Astonished, Peter says, "Lord, are you washing my feet?. . . You shall never wash my feet!" Jesus answers, "If I do not wash you, you have no part with me." Confused, Peter responds, "Lord, not my feet only, but also my hands and my head." In other words, "Lord, give me a bath!" Jesus explains, "He who is bathed needs only to wash his feet, but is completely clean."

What a dear, confused disciple. Peter was so full of himself that he couldn't see the simplest needs clearly. "I have given you an example," Jesus says, "that you should do as I have done to you. Most assuredly, I say to you, a servant is not greater than his master; nor is he who is sent greater than he who sent him. If you know these things, happy are you if you do them."

Do you want to be happy? Jesus tells us how: Take the role of a servant. He is not saying specifically that we therefore need to have foot-washing services. We likely do not have the same needs in our gatherings that they had in that upper room. They had come in from walking barefoot or with open-toe sandals on dung-strewn streets, to sit down with their feet adjacent to the next person's face. Our ways are different. But just as they had a need, so people around us have needs that we are able to meet. The question is, Will we use the resources we have to meet what needs we can, and thereby know real happiness?

Listen to Paul, who captured the issue beautifully:

> Let nothing be done through selfish ambition or conceit, but in lowliness of mind let each esteem others better than himself. Let each of you look out not only for his own interests, but also for the interests of others. Let this mind be in you which was also in Christ Jesus . . . (Philippians 2:3-5).

JESUS PROCLAIMING THE TRUTH

Now back to Jesus' use of the Word: He began by giving a demonstration of the truth. It proved to be more than one of them—Judas—could handle, and he left. By the end of chapter 13, the group of disciples in the upper room is down to the real core, whom Jesus calls "little children."

> Little children, I shall be with you a little while longer. You will seek me, and as I said to the Jews, "Where I am going you cannot come," so now I say to you. (13:33)

Now we move from demonstration of truth to proclamation of truth: "A new commandment I give to you, that you love one another. As I have loved you, that you also love one another" (13:34). What love is Jesus referring to? Don't race ahead to the Cross. That had not yet taken place, and is not the love He is speaking of. Jesus is saying, "As I *have loved* you . . ." How had He loved them? He took the role of a servant and did for them the thing He could do that needed to be done. He loved them not only in word—as important as words are—but also in action.

Notice how extremely important this is to Christ's kingdom advance: "By this," Jesus says, "will all men know that you are My disciples, that you love one another" (13:35). In thirty-five years of preaching throughout this country, I have yet to find a church that has taken John 13:34-35 as its evangelistic commission for even a year—really strategizing to put this truth into practice. Our concern goes so directly to reaching "all men" that we forget how Jesus said they would be reached.

It was a short sermon, and extremely profound: "Peter, love Andrew, and everyone will know you are Mine; James, love John, and Simon, love Matthew, and all men will know you belong to Me."

Jesus didn't say anything to them about loving "all men." In fact, in the Lord's Prayer of John 17 He says, "I pray not for the world. I pray for those whom Thou hast given Me." The key to reaching the world would be found in the eleven loving each other.

Peter's response to this magnificent truth—a task that would cost no money and would not need the media, but that would be effective in reaching a world—was to summarily dismiss it without acknowledging it. "Lord," he says, "where are you going?"—a reaction no more irrelevant than many of our responses today after receiving God's Word: "Who's playing on TV this afternoon?"

Jesus could have said, "Peter, you don't catch on too fast, do you? For the third time, I'll tell you: Where I'm going, you can't go." Rather, Jesus is the epitome of patience: "Where I'm going, you cannot follow me now, but you shall follow me afterwards."

Then a second question from Peter: "Lord, why can't I follow you now?" Sounds just like our children: You tell them they can't go, and the next question is "Why?" And if you dare to explain that they are really not able to go, or the task is more than they can handle, then they begin to flex their muscles and say, "I *am* able! You misunderstand me, Dad. I am able!" That's exactly what Peter did—and he wasn't alone, though he happened to be the mouthpiece. He was the preacher, and he stuck his foot squarely in his mouth: "Lord, I will lay down my life for Your sake! You misunderstand me, Lord. You really don't know the measure of my commitment. I am so committed, I'll die for You."

Not only did Peter not know the measure of his commitment, but he also had the audacity to contradict Jesus. He really knew neither himself nor his Lord! Out of his finiteness he sought to correct the infinite Son of God. Thus Jesus was forced to unveil to Peter what he was really like. "Will you lay down your life for My sake? Most assuredly I say to you, the rooster shall not crow until you have denied Me three times."

What a devastating blast that revelation must have been to Peter. Just think of being denuded spiritually in front of your closest colleagues—especially if you are their spokesman. Out of all the sins the disciples might conceive of, none could be more despicable than to deny Christ, after all He had done for them, and would yet do. Yet now they knew that before the night was over, Peter would deny three times that he knew Him.

The Lord could have expanded that so vividly. Others might have added, "You've got a big mouth, Peter—lots of talk but not much action." Jesus, Who knew all that Peter would do, said only enough to bring conviction. What grace! How true to the prophecy of Isaiah:

> "A bruised reed He will not break,
> And smoking flax He will not quench."
>   (Isaiah 42:3, cf. Matthew 12:20)

Luke records more of Jesus' words: "Simon, Simon, Satan has desired to have you [he is lusting after you, licking his chops for you] but I have prayed for you [and Jesus' prayers never go unanswered] that your faith fail not. And when you get turned around [not *if*, but *when*] strengthen your brethren [pick up the pieces with those who have stumbled along the way, because they followed your example]."

Following Jesus' response to Peter's boast at the end of John 13, He continues by saying (and I believe I will never, in all my life, get over this), "Let not your heart be troubled." If I were Peter, I would say, "O Lord, what do You mean? If what You have just said is true, how can You tell me to let not my heart be troubled? Lord, take my life now before I do it!"

"Let not your heart be troubled," Jesus comforts. Then He takes them to the most important thing in the world for Christian action: right thinking about what God is like. Do you remember Daniel's words? "They that do know their God shall be strong and take action" (Daniel 11:32). I do what I do, because I think like I think. Friar Lawrence was right on target in *Practicing the Presence of God* when he said, "Counting upon God as being never absent would be holiness complete." Whenever I do a wrong thing, whenever I sin, it is precisely and ultimately because I am thinking wrong about what God is like. Every sin is ultimately a failure to think right about God. And Peter was spending more time looking at himself and his own expertise than he was looking at what God is like. He was a good twentieth-century navel-gazer, seeking the "self-esteem" that starts anthropocentrically rather than theocentrically. God knows we don't need more people seeking to love themselves today. We need more people seeking to love God. And if I will find out what God is like, I will be lifted, I will gain self-worth, because I am made in the image of God. The greater my God becomes, the higher I will rise. The deeper, the higher, the wider, the more majestic my concept is of my God, the more vital and powerful will be my relationship to Him.

Hear the words of Philip Keller in *A Shepherd Looks at Psalm Twenty-Three*:

> So when the simple—though sublime—statement is made by a man or woman that "the Lord is my Shepherd," it immediately implies a profound yet practical working relationship between a human being and his Maker. It links a lump of common clay to divine destiny—it means a mere mortal becomes the cherished object of divine diligence.
>
> This thought alone should stir my spirit, quicken my own sense of awareness, and lend enormous dignity to myself as an individual. To think that God in Christ is deeply concerned about me as a particular person immediately gives great purpose and enormous meaning to my short sojourn upon this planet. And the greater, the wider, the more majestic my concept is of the Christ—the more vital will be my relationship to Him. Obviously, David, in this Psalm, is speaking not as the shepherd, though he was one, but as a sheep; one of the flock. He spoke with a strong sense of pride and devotion and admiration. It was as though he literally boasted aloud, "Look at who my shepherd is—my owner—my manager! The Lord is!
>
> After all, he knew from firsthand experience that the lot in life of any particular sheep depended on the type of man who owned it. Some men were gentle, kind, intelligent, brave and selfless in their devotion to their stock. Under one man sheep would struggle, starve and

suffer endless hardship. In another's care they would flourish and thrive contentedly. So if the Lord is my Shepherd I should know something of His character and understand something of His ability. To meditate on this I frequently go out at night to walk alone under the stars and remind myself of His majesty and might. Looking up at the star-studded sky I remember that at least 250,000,000 x 250,000,000 such bodies—each larger than our sun, one of the smallest of the stars—have been scattered across the vast spaces of the universe by His hand. I recall that the planet earth, which is my temporary home for a few short years, is so minute a speck of matter in space that if it were possible to transport our most powerful telescope to our nearest neighbor star, Alpha Centauri, and look back this way, the earth could not be seen, even with the aid of that powerful instrument. All this is a bit humbling. It drains the "ego" from a man and puts things in proper perspective. It makes me see myself as a mere mite of material in an enormous universe. Yet the staggering fact remains that Christ the Creator of such an enormous universe of overwhelming magnitude, deigns to call Himself my Shepherd and invites me to consider myself His sheep—His special object of affection and attention. Who better could care for me?[2]

Jesus, knowing this perfectly, proceeds to deepen Peter's understanding of God. And so, Jesus says, "Don't let your heart be troubled, Peter. Don't be loosed from your moorings. Hang on to what you know about God and I am going to give you much more to trust. Believe in God! Believe also in Me."

Thus, He begins to tell Peter and the others about God. He does not proceed to expand the nature and dimensions of Peter's sin. You do not whip a jaded horse. Remember, it was prophesied of Jesus that He would not quench the smoking flax and He would not break the bruised reed. He did not shoot His wounded. And knowing all that He knew about Peter and what he would do, and having exposed just a little bit of it,

Jesus now proceeds to correct Peter's anemic thinking, because he has been believing a lie, especially about himself and his ability. God the Son is going to correct that with truth. Propositional truth! In John 14, Jesus begins the procedure of lifting Peter and the others with words—words of truth.

And what does He say? Of all things, He begins with eschatology. "In my Father's house are many dwelling places. If it were not so, I would have told you. I go to prepare a place for you. And if I go and prepare a place for you I will come again and receive you unto myself that where I am, there you may be also."

Can you imagine Peter's thinking now?

"Me, Lord? Wait a minute, Lord. You just got through saying that before the night is out I am going to deny You three times. There is a place for people like me?"

But Jesus said, "I will come again and receive you to Myself that where I am, there you may be also."

"Me, Lord?"

"You, Peter. You, Andrew. You, James. You, John." Jesus practiced unconditional love, whereas they lived in the midst of a world system of conditional love. Paul catches the truth of this in his "much more's" of Romans 5:8-10.

Then Jesus goes on to tell them about the Father. Twenty-three times in John 14 He mentions the name of the Father. No place in the entire Word of God has as much reference to the Father. But He not only tells them about the Father, He tells them more about the Son, and He tells them about the Spirit—*God the Father! God the Son! God the Holy Spirit!* Do you think Theology Proper is practical? Jesus did. He gave them a short discourse on Theology Proper. At the time of their deepest need, when Peter was at the bottom of the pits, He didn't whip him. He lifted him with truth, as He does all the way through chapter 14.

JESUS ILLUSTRATING THE TRUTH

Following Jesus' proclamation of truth to His disciples in the upper room, He led His small band out into the night, across the Kidron Valley to the Garden of Gethsemane. Somewhere enroute, He sought to reinforce His proclamation of truth with a vivid illustration from the vineyard. His order of teaching was "demonstration, proclamation, and illustration." The illustration He here used was an extended metaphor.

To properly understand this figure of speech, we need to recall that Jesus did not use figures merely for color or entertainment, but to emphasize or underscore specific truths. As our doctrine of inerrancy of the Word reminds us of the veracity of every part of the Word, it does not allow a free-wheeling interpretation that provokes a fluid imagination. If we come up with six different interpretations, you can bank on it, five of them are wrong. All six, in fact, may be wrong. Energetic Bible-thumping doesn't add an extra interpretation. We can be sure that God doesn't stutter or speak mysteries to be unravelled in a variety of ways. Whether by figures or plain literal language, Jesus spoke for the purpose of being understood.

Our problem in understanding this passage today is that we know so little about vineyards. We need to reconstruct that ancient setting and note what Jesus said as He looked at the grapevine: "I am the true vine, and My Father is the vinedresser. Every branch in Me that does not bear fruit, He takes away. And every branch that bears fruit, he prunes it, that it may bear more fruit. You are already clean because of the Word which I have spoken unto you."

Jesus here illustrates the action of the Father by means of a metaphor from viticulture. A vineyard requires harder and more regular labor than any other form of agriculture and thus becomes a fitting analogy to the process of the Father in bringing His children to maturity in Christ. Now how does God my Father deal with me? Jesus says that the first thing the Father does is to take the branch that isn't bearing fruit and *airo* it.

Now the most basic meaning in any Greek lexicon for *airo* is "to lift, to bear or to carry." And if you take Gerhard Kittel's *Theological Dictionary of the New Testament*, the largest lexical work ever compiled, and look under *airo*, you find that the very first listing is "to lift up from the ground".[3] And that is as basic to this passage as you can get, because that very basic usage of the term fits right into the viticultural setting that Jesus and the eleven are looking at. "Every branch in Me not bearing fruit, He lifts up from the ground." This helps to understand the rendering "takes away" in most translations—that is, He takes the branch away from the ground.

This process was brought home to me very vividly on several trips to Israel. When you travel south from Jerusalem past Bethlehem to Hebron, you see mile after mile of grapevines bending down to the ground. In Israel, unlike the United States, the stalks of grape vines are, for the most part, down on the ground during the nonproductive season—not bearing fruit. But when the time comes for fruit, the vinedressers begin to lift them off the ground. And today, two thousand years later, you can see the vine-tenders on the West Bank of the Jordan doing it the same way they did it then. They get a rock (about eight to ten inches high), pick up the stalk and put the rock under the top end of the stalk. Then they go to the next one and do the same thing.

Several days later they come back and move that rock back a little further toward the root and do the same to every stalk in the vineyard. Several days later they will repeat the process until they get that stalk positioned properly for fruit-bearing. In the process, the branches have been "taken away" or "lifted" from the ground. One may wonder why they need to lift the branches away from the ground. By doing this they control the exposure of the grapes to the sun. The further they lift the branches, the more exposure the fruit gets.[4] Furthermore, if they leave the stalk on the ground, the branches will shoot tiny roots directly from the branch into the top surface of the earth where there is very little moisture. They will produce grapes—little hard, sour grapes. But if they lift that stalk off the ground, those branches will get their sustenance from the stalk whose deep roots go into the rich moisture of the earth, and they will produce the succulent fruit for which Israel is known.

John Mitchell has caught the point beautifully in his commentary, *An Everlasting Love*:

> "Every branch in me that beareth not fruit he taketh away." The primary meaning of the Greek here is "to raise up," not "to take away." Verse two should read this way: "Every branch in Me that does not bear fruit He raises up." What is the purpose of the husbandman? He goes through the vineyard looking for fruit. But here is a branch on the ground, not bearing any fruit. What does he do? Cut it off? No. He raises it up, so the sun can shine upon it, and the air can get to it. Then it will bear fruit.
>
> Some Christians don't bear fruit. What's the matter with them? They need to have the Son shining on them. When a believer is out of fellowship with God and is occupied with the things of the world, he is not bearing fruit. The husbandman must come along and lift the branch, raising it up and bringing the individual believer back into fellowship in order that he or she might bear fruit. God's purpose is to gather fruit, not render judgment.[5]

What a beautiful picture Jesus gave His disciples! We can understand why He prayed later, "I do not pray that You should take them out of the world, but that You should keep them out of the evil one" (John 17:15). Here is a compound form of *airo*, namely *epairo*, and it is in the aorist tense rather than the present tense as in John 15:2. Jesus does not want the Father to lift[6] them completely out of the world, but to keep on lifting them away from the earth. Thus, Jesus says, "I want them in the world." Do you see it? "I want them in the world—but not of it; in it, but not deriving their sustenance from it." The sustenance of the branches (believers) is to be from the vine (Christ), not from the evil world system.

On another occasion Jesus used another figure of speech to teach this same group the same principle. "I send you forth," Jesus said, "as sheep in the midst of wolves" (Matthew 10:16). If you give that even a moment's thought, you will recognize what an impossible position that is. Sheep cannot naturally exist in the midst of wolves. "In" wolves, perhaps, but not "in the midst of." That requires outside protection. So it is with us. But when we are in that position, we tend to accommodate ourselves to our surroundings and become like the wolves—like the world system. And we lose our testimony to the world around us. Thus, the Father lifts us into the light and away from the dirt.

Now, what else does the Father do? Not only does He pursue a process of carefully and progressively lifting the branches into positions suitable for developing and ripening fruit (which is what was being done for Peter and the others all through chapter 14), but when the branch bears fruit, the Father purges (*kathairo*) it.

Once again, most of our translations completely miss the viticultural point by translating *kathairo* by the word "prune." A little reflection will remind you that no vinedresser goes out in the vineyard to begin cutting off branches once the fruit is on them. If he did, the vines would bleed to death because the sap is running strongly when the fruit is on the branches. The KJV is closer in its use of "purge," but the Berkeley and Weymouth translations are best with the use of "cleanse." The old verb *kathairo* occurs in the New Testament only in John 15:2, but the related adjective, *katharos*, is in verse 3 as well as twenty-three other times in the New Testament.

In *A New Testament Wordbook*, William Barclay describes *katharos* as "one of the great Greek words." It basically describes something which is pure from every taint and admixture of evil. One of the most familiar uses is in the Beatitudes. "Blessed are the pure in heart, for they shall see God" (Matthew 5:8). After comparing *katharos* with the words it is closely associated with, Barclay expands it this way: "Blessed are those whose motives are absolutely unmixed, whose minds are utterly sincere, who are completely and totally single-minded."

In the light of the foregoing, if "pruning" is not what a vinedresser does to fruit-bearing branches, what does he do? Once the fruit is on the vine, there is the problem of pests: "The leafhopper, grape-berry moth, and the grape rootworm attack the vines. The grape-berry moth makes grapes wormy. Four fungi that destroy grapes are powdery mildew, downy mildew, black rot, and anathracnose."[7]

Today, we control insect and fungus pests with dusts and sprays which they didn't have in ancient times. We do not know precisely what the vinedresser used to keep the fruit clean and free from pests and fungi, but we do know what the Divine Vinedresser uses because He tells us in verse 3: "Now you are clean through the Word which I have spoken unto you." As has been already noted, *kathairei* ("cleanse" or "purge") of verse 2 and *katharoi* ("clean" or "purge") of verse 3 are from the same root. Jesus looks upon them as clean, and the vital cause and souce of their cleansing, Jesus said, is "the Word which I have spoken to you."

There is no need to search further for that "Word" than what we have in the preceding discourse in the upper room. Jesus gave them the precious, cleansing words of revelation about the character and work of the triune God.

Notice how Jesus had focused on the Person and work of God the Father, God the Son, and God the Holy Spirit. Why? Because of the basic principle of right thinking. A person's actions are the outworking of his deepest thoughts. "As a man thinks in his heart, so is he" (Proverbs 23:7). Right thinking is indispensable to right acting. And right thinking begins by thinking right about God. Solomon had it right:

> Wisdom is the principal thing;
> Therefore get wisdom.
> And in all your getting, get understanding.
> Exalt her, and she will promote you;
> She will bring you honor, when you embrace her.
> She will place on your head an ornament of grace;
> A crown of glory she will deliver to you.
>   (Proverbs 4:7-9)

Again, he says, "The fear of the LORD is the beginning of wisdom, and the knowledge of the Holy One is understanding" (Proverbs 9:10).

Listen to God's Word to Jeremiah:

> Thus says the LORD: "Let not the wise man glory in his
> wisdom, let not the mighty man glory in his might, nor
> let the rich man glory in his riches; but let him who
> glories glory in this, that he understands and knows Me,
> that I am the LORD, exercising lovingkindness, judgment,
> and righteousness in the earth. For in these I delight,"
> says the LORD. (Jeremiah 9:23-24)

Again, after proving this truth for a lifetime, Daniel exclaimed, "The people who know their God shall be strong, and carry out great exploits" (Daniel 11:32).

Because Jesus operated totally by the truth of this principle, He knew exactly the root of Peter's actions—wrong thinking about God. So He provided the revelatory truths that would be the source of cleansing.

What potential that planted in Peter's mind! And Jesus watered the seed of the Word with prayer as He had promised to do (Luke 22:32). "Father, sanctify them with Thy truth. Thy word is truth" (John 17:17). One cannot but recall the question in the matchless Psalm 119: "How can a young man cleanse his way? By taking heed according to Your word" (119:9).

Now, what must Peter and the disciples do about this truth in order to experience the benefits of it? The answer to this is found in John 15:4-5. But first, notice carefully the

change in pronouns. The active agent in verse 2 is "He"—the
Father. Now in verse 4 the action shifts to "you"—the disciples
(who were striving with each other to be the greatest and would
all stumble that very night).

How would these disciples be delivered from their petti-
ness, egotism, and hypocrisy? Listen, as Jesus introduces a
new word into the discourse: "Abide in me, and I in you."

Nine times Jesus uses "abide" in verses 4-10. It has the
basic idea of staying in a given place, state, relation or expec-
tancy. "To stand fast" catches the idea. Having heard the great
truths that Jesus gave them, they need to settle down in them,
to believe them with all their heart; then they will become
progressively more fruitful.

Remember the words of Jesus in John 8:31-32. To those
who believed Him, Jesus said: "If you abide in My word, you
are My disciples indeed. And you shall know the truth, and
the truth shall make you free." The word "abide" indicates a
constancy of belief in relation to Christ and His Word.

Commenting on John 15:4-5, Lewis Sperry Chafer states:

> . . . the word of exhortation directs the believer to remain
> in communion with Christ as He remained in communion
> with His Father. As the sap flows from the vine into the
> branch that remains in contact, so the spiritual vitality
> flows from Christ to the believer who abides.[8]

I hear some people today demeaning simple belief by
calling it "easy believism" and I sometimes wonder if they
prefer "hard believism." I appreciate the pastor who countered
the "easy believism" objection with, "Not only is it easy, it is
free."

God made it as simple as possible. The Lord says, "Just
believe. Believe what I have said about Myself and My will
for you." (John 14:1). But I can identify with that fellow who
said, "Lord, I believe. Help my unbelief" (Mark 9:24). I find
at times that it is hard to believe. Jesus is not saying, "Do
something about it," He is saying, "Believe it—believe it, and

something will be done about it. But you must believe it. Settle down in it."

One of my favorite illustrations of this truth is from my days as a chaplain in the U. S. Navy, when a "white hat" was trying to convince me I needed to learn how to swim. "Chaplain," he said, "one of these days they are going to drop you in the ocean, and you're going to be gone." So one Sunday afternoon after chapel I said, "Okay, Wayne, you can teach me how to swim today."

As we walked to the pool, he said, "Now, Chaplain, there is just one thing you have to remember: The hardest thing about swimming is getting over the fear of the water. If you can just get over the fear of the water, you won't have any problem at all." That sounded simple enough.

Once we were at the pool he said, "Now, lie down on the water." I tried to do exactly what he said, and I went directly to the bottom. They pulled me up, kicking and sputtering. "Okay," he said, "everybody can make a mistake once; now let's try it again, Chaplain. Just lie down on the water." I again went directly to the bottom. This went on a number of times until it was becoming apparent that I was losing the joy.

Once more he said, "Now, Chaplain, I want you to just lie down on . . ."

"Listen, Wayne," I interrupted. "You keep telling me to lie down on the water, and I keep trying to lie down on the water, and every time I try I go right to the bottom!" He looked at me, still smiling through clenched teeth. After all, I was an officer and he was a white-hat. "Chaplain," he said, "that's just what's wrong with you. I keep telling you to lie down on the water, and you keep *trying* to lie on the water; now will you quit *trying* to lie on the water, and just lie on the water!"

Now you may think there is little difference between *trying* to lie on the water and actually lying on the water, but for me that was the difference between the top of the water and the bottom of the water. I found it all had to do with one thing: Thinking! Attitude! When I thought the water would drown me, I pushed my arms down, and the further I pushed them, the further down they went. I tried to hold my head up out of the water, and the more I held it up, the farther down it went. When I changed my attitude toward the water, however, and I let my arms come up and my head go back, the same water that was drowning me was now holding me up. The water hadn't changed one iota. The only thing that changed was my thinking and consequent attitude toward the water.

Many people have that same problem with God. Their idea of God is drowning them. God is not drowning them, but *their idea* of God is drowning them. They are believing the devil's idea about God, just as Peter did. Can you believe how difficult it must have been for Peter to understand the unconditional love of Jesus Christ at this point? Why, he didn't operate that way! Can you believe the faithfulness of Jesus at this point? Peter had to see that. And Jesus said to him, "Now, you are clean, you are purged through the Word I have spoken unto you." Does that mean Peter immediately started acting right? No, he was still acting in the flesh in chapter 18—drawing his sword and whipping off Malchus' ear. Jesus had to get him to put his sword back again and give him another insight on His Person and power (cf. Matthew 26:53). But Peter didn't do that anymore in Acts (cf. Acts 4:19-20). Why? Because he had come to know who Jesus is and, consequently, who he was in relation to Jesus Christ.

Furthermore, he knew where he was going. And they couldn't intimidate him anymore. Why? John answers, "Perfect love casts out fear" (1 John 4:18). When Peter was told "Don't speak in that name again," he doesn't whip out his sword and say, "Oh, yeah. You dirty bullies! You and who else is going to stop me? Let's have at it!" No, he says, "We ought to obey God rather than men." We know Who is final authority. We'll take our chances with Him.

Coolly and calmly Peter did it. And one day he became a martyr. That shouldn't come as a surprise. Jesus said, "They hated me—don't be surprised if they hate you" (cf. John 15:18).

If you are distinct . . . if you really stand out . . . if you are
in the world but not of it . . . if you are sheep in the midst of
wolves . . . your fruit of Christlikeness will stand out and you
will prove to be Christ's disciple (cf. 15:8). Some will despise
you even as they did Christ, but some will believe because of
your fruit.

But, you say, "What about verse 6?" Well, look at it:

> If anyone does not abide in Me, he is cast out as a branch
> and is withered; and they gather them and throw them
> into the fire, and they are burned.

First, notice the change in pronouns once again. We have
moved from "He" (the Father acting on the believers) in verse
2, to "you" (the believers being exhorted by Jesus to abide)
in verses 4-5, to "they" in verse 6—the twofold reponse on
the part of those outside of Christ to what they see in believers'
lives. The unbelievers in verse 6 are "they" who don't see any
fruit from the one who is not abiding, and so what do they
conclude? There is nothing to them! They are hypocrites. In
effect, they cast them out, throw them in the fire and burn them.

And often that is what they conclude about us. That's
what the world says: "You are just a bunch of phonies. You
are just another religion. You don't really show me what Jesus
said would be seen in John 13:34-35." An attorney friend of
mine said to me recently, "The world doesn't have to lie about
the church today. All they have to do is tell the truth." That is
verse 6!

You see, in verses 6-8 you have come full circle from the
first statement of the Christian's greatest apologetic. If you
want to really see this, just compare 13:35 with 15:8—

> By this, all will know that you are My disciples if you
> have love one to another. (13:35)

In 15:8, Jesus says metaphorically the same thing:

> By this My Father is glorified that you bear much fruit
> and so prove to be My disciples.

Prove to whom? To the "they" of verse 6—those who need to see Jesus Christ in us.

If I wanted to translate 13:35 metaphorically, I would say, "By this all will know that you are my disciples, that you 'fruit' one another." Or, "A new commandment I give unto you that you 'fruit' one another, as I have 'fruited' you, that you also 'fruit' one another. And by this 'fruit' all men will know that you are my disciples." But He is not speaking metaphorically in John 13:35-36; He is speaking in a plain, literal way there, while in John 15 He illustrates it metaphorically. He cinches it vividly because this is the key to outreach for Jesus Christ.

What a powerful statement: "Now you are clean . . . " Through what? "The Word."

The Word. The Word which is truth.

Thus Jesus applies the authority of the Word which is truth.

NOTES

1. See Earl D. Radmacher, *You and Your Thoughts: The Power of Right Thinking* (Tyndale House, 1977).

2. Phillip Keller, *A Shepherd Looks at Psalm Twenty-Three* (Zondervan, 1970), pp. 17-19.

3. Much confusion has arisen at this point because of misunderstanding of the traditional translation "takes away" without knowing the basic meaning of *airo*. The marginal note in the NKJV ("or lift up") is helpful whereas the NIV translation ("cuts off") unfortunately misses the point entirely. If John wanted to say the latter, he had a good word for it, *apokopto*, which he uses later to record Peter's action when he "cut off" the right ear of Malchus (John 18:10 and 18:26).

4. Cf. A. C. Schultz, "Vine, Vineyard," vol. 5, p. 882, in *The Zondervan Pictorial Encyclopedia of the Bible*, Merrill C. Tenney, editor. "Too much exposure to the sun in the early period of the growth of the clusters would cause the grapes to ripen before they were fully grown."

5. John G. Mitchell, *An Everlasting Love: A Devotional Study of the Gospel of John* (Multnomah Press, 1982).

6. The same word is used of the ascension of Christ in Acts 1:9.

7. *World Book Encyclopedia*, vol. 7, p. 312.

8. Lewis Sperry Chafer, *Systematic Theology*, vol. VII, p. 3.

The very foundation of Christian faith relies upon the Word of God being ultimate, changeless truth. However, "One of the amazing departures of biblical thought in any age is that a person is often thought to be wise, not on the basis of what he affirms, but on the basis of what he denies. The first concept to be denied by the falsely wise is the very notion of God."

That statement, from a book by Ronald B. Allen, draws our attention to something which is recurrent throughout the pages of Scripture: the contrast between the infinite wisdom of God and the meager worldly-wisdom of man. It is a theme illustrated in the Proverbs, where Madame Folly's role as antagonist is played out in contrast to that of the protagonist, Lady Wisdom. We see this expressed also in 1 Corinthians 1:20: "Consider what have the philosopher, the writer, the critic of this world to show for all their wisdom. Has not God made the wisdom of the world look foolish?"

Dr. Ronald B. Allen, *professor of Hebrew Scripture at Western Seminary, focuses upon the Word as the very light of God, the Word as unique wisdom.*

C H A P T E R   2

THE WORD AS DIVINE LIGHT:
Its Unique Wisdom

RONALD B. ALLEN

THE United Methodist church is in trouble. Though still a very large Protestant denomination in America, its membership and attendance levels are slipping so fast some are wondering how long that church will survive.

These alarmist words are not from an enemy, but from one who loves his church and is one of its leaders. The bishop of the Arkansas area of the United Methodist church has written a highly critical evaluation of the state of his church. Bishop Richard B. Wilke's book asks the lamentable question, *And Are We Yet Alive?* A reading of the book leaves one with the uneasy answer to the rhetorical question in the title: Perhaps, but only barely.

Bishop Wilke's book should be read not only by Methodists but by leaders and concerned members of many Protestant denominations. That which ails the United Methodists is a common ailment, affecting Baptists and Presbyterians as well.

THE NEED FOR CLEAR FOCUS

Wilke describes a church that has lost its focus, that is involved in ministries of social service and political activism, but apart from a conscious determination to spread the gospel of the Lord Jesus Christ. He points to administrative desires for perfectly balanced representation on denominational boards, with little corresponding concern for discipleship. Something is askew, he says, when a church has more administrative staff members serving on committees than missionaries serving on the battle fronts of the faith.

Bishop Wilke does offer hope to his reader, but only if the church he serves and loves will be willing to make radical changes. He calls for a return of focus, a new center on the Person of God and a renewed commitment to the Scriptures. He points to the scriptural demands for reaching out to lost people with the gospel of Jesus Christ in new and innovative ways. He speaks of the United States of America as one of the hardest mission fields of all, a field the church dare not neglect.

Are we yet alive? Perhaps. But not for long, unless real changes are made.

I applaud Bishop Wilke for his book, and have been moved by reading the book to renew prayer for godly men and women in the mainline churches who really do wish their churches to return to center and to restore a focus on what the church is really about in God's world.

At the same time, Bishop Wilke disappointed me when he spoke of his desire to return to the Bible. For he did not present an inerrant Scripture as the Bible he wished to embrace. In fact he makes a point of the matter. He speaks of wishing his denomination to be a biblical people, but avers, "We are not fundamentalists, not literalists, not inerrancy addicts. . . . The word *inerrancy* is not a biblical word. . . . While we do not take the Bible literally, we must take it seriously. . . . Without the authority of the Bible, we have no authority at all" (pp. 87-88).

The reform of Bishop Wilke is a good reform. The question I have is whether it is good enough. Is it good enough to return to a Bible that is not inerrant to reform a church that has wandered from Scripture?

And what is the view of God in such a setting?

It is my belief that a right view of the Scriptures begins with a right view of God. Yet we gain a right view of God only as we come to Him through the Scriptures. Our view of God and our view of Scripture interplay with each other. Elevate the one and we elevate the other. For the Scripture speaks of God and God speaks in Scripture.

We speak of the wisdom of the Scriptures because we know of the wisdom of God. And the more we read the Scriptures, the more we learn of the wisdom of God. He is "immortal, invisible, God only wise," and because God is wise we believe the Scriptures to be wise.

In this book we are seeking to elevate the Word of God. But we are not just lifting high a book. Rather, by holding the book high we are elevating the Person of our God.

A Song of Wisdom for Difficult Times

A particularly splendid passage in the Psalms describes God's wisdom, and hence, the wisdom of the Word. Psalm 147 was written at a time when the people of God were discouraged and distraught. They had returned to the land, but things were not as they thought they might be. The walls of the city were rebuilt, but they were not the great walls of Israel's past. They would keep out brigands, but they were still a part of foreign domination. The new temple was built, but those who had some memory of the building it replaced wept at the comparison. *These puny walls. That little building. This miserable people. Oh, for the great and glorious days of old!*

To such a people came the encouraging words of the psalmist who taught them to praise God, a good and pleasant thing, even a matter of beauty (verse 1). Then he reminded them that the very things they seemed to disparage were in fact the works of God. It is Yahweh who is building the walls. It is the Lord who is bringing His people back. It is the Savior who mends the brokennesses of His people.

If any good thing is being done, it is being done by the Lord. Rather than look back with nostalgia to the olden days, the psalmist urges them to capture a new vision of the grandeur of God who surpasses any day!

NAMING THE STARS

The psalmist reflects on the galaxies of heaven and sings:

He counts the number of the stars;
He counts them all by name. (147:4)

Think of it! Our God knows the number of the stars. He knows them each by name.

Our view of the universe is greatly expanded over that of people in the ancient day in which this psalm was first sung. Today we believe that our galaxy, the Milky Way, contains more than 100 billion stars—and God knows them all! Our galaxy is one of perhaps 100 billion galaxies—and God knows their names!

I have trouble with names in a class. Sometimes even in my family, I'll call one son by the other's name. And sometimes I do not even know the names of my goats!

Several years ago our family was preparing to go on a sabbatical trip to Asia, and we had to farm out our farm. We sent the rabbits with one person, the chickens with another. The couple who were to stay in our house agreed to take care of the horse and the dog. But what about the three milking goats?

The woman who had planned to care for them found that a family problem would not allow it. She told us on the Thursday of the week we were leaving. Saturday morning we would fly to Manila. But we wondered what could we do with our goats? You really learn who your friends are when you have three goats that need milking . . .

At the time I was taking the *Dairy Goat Journal* (there are magazines for everything). I took a copy and began reading the ads. Then I prayed that God would give direction, and I called the first number.

The woman who answered had a goat farm in Canby. When I told her my name and my problem, she said, "Oh, I can't take care of your goats. Do you know how many goats I have?" I had no idea. She had about fifty, if I remember correctly. She simply could not take care of three more.

I was about to ask if she knew of someone who might be able to do this for me. She interrupted, "Wait a minute. What are their names?" I couldn't believe it. *What are their names? What did that matter?*

"They do have names, don't they?" she said.

"Sure, but the names are a bit silly."

"Well, tell me."

"The first goat, uh, her name is Coco-Puff."

"You have Coco-Puff?"

"Yes."

"Is she the real Coco-Puff?"

"The only one I know."

"Well, who were her dam and sire?"

"I don't know."

"Well, go get her papers. You do have papers?"

When I returned to the phone, she recited quickly to me three sets of ancestors on both sides. I couldn't believe it. I had called her at random, yet she knew the complete pedigree of my goat.

"What's the next one?"

"She's Jeckmate."

"Oh," she said, "I know her." And she gave me three generations on both sides of Jeckmate.

"And the third?"

Now I was getting in to this. "Shanty's Fleet."

"Shanty's Fleet. I don't know her."

"You don't know her? Well her mother is . . ." I went on, reading from the papers.

"Oh. I know her mother!"

The upshot is that she was more than happy to care for my goats. Because, as she said, "I *know* them."

And my God knows the stars!

HIS INFINITE UNDERSTANDING

The fifth verse of Psalm 147 tells us that the understanding of Yahweh is infinite. The Hebrew reads *litvunato 'en mispar,* "of his understanding there is no number." While He is able to number the stars, there is no number to quantify His wisdom.

And it is the wisdom of God we confront when we turn to the Scriptures. It is particularly in the Book of Proverbs that we are drawn to think of the wisdom of God, and hence, of the wisdom of the Word.

I recently started wearing a diamond ring that was my father's when he was a pianist. He gave it to me over twenty years ago, but I have worn it only now and then. The ring has a modest diamond braced in a silver fitting and backed by black onyx. This same diamond would be unnoticed in a drawer filled with stones. But against the black setting it stands out and is resilient.

There is so much to the wonder and majesty of God that we might find our view of Him unclear at times. We might be so dazzled by one attribute that we miss another.

In Proverbs, His wisdom is singled out for special display, as a diamond set against a dark, lustrous background. The portrait of Lady Wisdom in Proverbs 1-9 is a way to describe the wisdom of God in a remarkably compelling manner.

As we look at Lady Wisdom, we think of the wisdom of the Word of God. For the Lady is Torah walking.

As we look at Lady Wisdom, we come to face the divine light of the Word.

As we look at Lady Wisdom, we confront the wisdom of God.

As we look at Lady Wisdom, we also learn to think of our Savior, the Lord Jesus in Whom are hidden all the treasures of wisdom and knowledge.

Let's look at her in this drama, and as we do, think of the Word and think of the Lord. She portrays both.

THE BUSY CITY

Imagine yourself in the city of ancient Jerusalem during the time of Solomon, her most opulent king. It is early morning on what promises to be a hot summer day. You are at an intersection. You find yourself benumbed by the business of the place.

People are moving about in every direction. Merchants call out to passers-by as they hawk their wares. Messengers sally. Priests rush. Tradesmen push. Urchins scurry. Families move, the little children harnessed to their elders so as not to be lost in the crowd. People mingle with animals and carts in the busy streets, all pressing about in every which way, and harlots linger, hoping for one more mark before calling the new day their night.

The street is filled with the sounds of people. All manner of people move before our view. Some are dressed with fine textures in bold colors. Most are in simple, drab fabrics. Some are in rags. Everywhere the people are talking, shouting, muttering, cursing. The warm, strong laryngeal sounds of Hebrew are heard most often. But here and there more exotic voices may be heard. As we turn toward the stranger sounds, we observe peoples from foreign lands, different from the rest by dress and look as well as sound. The capital of the Hebrews has become a truly cosmopolitan city. Peoples come from many nations. They come with their goods, their gods, and their notions. Most of all, they all seem to be talking.

Noise is everywhere. We hear the noise of people and their carts, of animal hoofs and brays, of clutter and dissonance, all bouncing about from one wall to another, echoing down corridors. Shakable things vibrate unexpectedly.

Then there is the air, weighted down with smells. If the air were a garden, the varieties of its plants would strain the classifying abilities of a botanist. The Elysian aroma of freshly baked bread commingles with the fetid odors of fresh animal droppings and stale urine. Smells of exotic foods cooking in small shops fight for position in the cluttered air. Fruits and vegetables are in open display, sending out their more delicate aromas. Stronger pungency comes from meats which hang from large hooks, and above the slabs of meat are the ever-circling flies. One waft of pleasing air is followed by a blast of noxious fumes, one clear odor is soon masked by a smell of uncertain origin.

But the people move so quickly, they seem hardly to notice these things. Only we, the visitors in this busy city, are really aware of all that we find about us. We are like all first-time visitors to the *suk*. We are stunned by motion, color, smell and sound. Even standing is a task; one must dodge the pressing bodies. Our senses overloaded, we barely cope with the scene.

THE EXQUISITE WOMAN

Of a sudden there comes something new—something so new, we cannot miss it. It is a Woman. The streets are filled with women and men, people are everywhere; but the presence of this Woman is felt. Though the early morning is already warm, there is a sense of dynamic warmth and presence in this Woman that reaches out and demands our response. She seems out of place, yet she is unembarrassed. Although she is unattended, no one would confuse her with one of the lurking harlots slumped at the entrance to the alley. This woman is a Lady.

Something about her is countercultural. Unquestionably feminine, she nevertheless moves boldly into this man's world of commerce. She stands with no child, is escorted by no husband, and has no father at her side, looking another direction while she blushes.

She is alone, boldly alone, yet unquestionably proper. Right in the middle of the concourse she takes her stand. People numbed to the business of the world about them take note of her. Simply put, the Lady is the loveliest woman we have ever seen. Then she speaks. In the tumult of this city, her voice is heard! The Lady's voice seems to come from another world. It is the voice of an angel, the sound of a god. Sweet, strong, resonant; it is a voice one loves at first hearing.

As she speaks, we distinguish her words. It seemed that nothing could surpass her beauty, but when we hear her words, we find them to eclipse even her appearance.

Her words are a call: To come to her. To reach out to her. To embrace her. To love her. To receive her gifts. To live with her forever.

VARIED RESPONSES TO WISDOM

Look at her there! The milling crowds have stopped. Sound is silenced; air is still. People are listening, puzzled at her words, stymied by her bold stance. She is simply not like other women we have known.

Then slowly, imperceptibly, the crowds begin to move again. They ignore her! They were as stunned as were we, but only for a moment. Now they are back to their business. They are talking again, the resounding tide of sound now drowning her words. Her arms are outstretched and the people brush by her on their way to market. The brief interruption the Lady has caused is soon forgotten. She is still there, but most ignore her. Merchants again call out to passers-by. Messengers sally. Priests rush. Tradesmen push. Urchins scurry. Families move, little children still in tow. They pass her by, their curiosity piqued only so slightly, but now on and about their business. Most go by her with barely another thought.

Perhaps the most amazing thing of all is to see a few young men turning directly from her, slinking into the alleys to find sleepy, love-wearied paramours. These young men seem nearly silly in their surreptitious attempts to fondle these too-compliant women as they haggle price and place. Some of these women are young and pretty—gifts so fragile, passing so quickly. But not all. One woman stands alone, deep in the shadows.

Nearby a door opens, sending an unexpected shaft of light down the alleyway. The light strikes another woman's face with an angry slap. We recoil at the sight of her. She seems to be evil itself. No one would confuse this woman with the proverbial harlot with the golden heart. Her wantonness is her religion, her waywardness her rites. Here is a confirmed wretch, an ordained priestess of sleaze. Her presence among the other harlots is as their queen; her degeneracy seems to be a portent of their future.

Even as the sad men approach them, the women stay in the shadows. They are night creatures and it is early day. Some hide out of shame, others attempting to hide the disfigurement of their faces and the more obvious disease of their bodies.

These fools haggle with harlots in the dimness of the alleyways when they might have embraced the Lady in the light! The Lady is still in the center of the street; young men turn their backs and slink into the alleys.

But wait! not all pass by the Lady. Here and there we notice young men who come close to her, reach out to her, embrace her . . . *and are transformed!*

RIGHT CHOICES

The choice of wisdom is to embrace the Lady. It is sheer folly to turn to a wanton streetwalker when one might have known the Lady.

In the Lady we approach the wisdom of God. We are also warned off from the folly of seeking another. It is as foolish to turn from God to an idol as to turn from the Lady to a trollop. The greater sadness is that people continue to make the same decisions they were making in Jerusalem nearly three thousand years ago.

People still turn from the Lady to their whores.

People still turn from life.

They choose death.

More people are in trouble today than just a particular denomination. All who turn from this Lady have chosen disaster. But all who turn to her will find life in her divine wisdom.

Bishop Wilke's question is a good one to ask of ourselves: Are WE yet alive?

May you in your reading of the Book of Wisdom decide all the more strongly for life.

Embrace the Lady.

Choose life!

Anniversary years are noted by distinctive symbols. It so happens that the diamond is the symbol for the sixtieth anniversary, celebrated by Western Conservative Baptist Seminary in 1987. Borrowing that image, in these pages we are taking the Word of God as a precious jewel and holding it up for examination and display so that its various facets can be appreciated.

In previous chapters we have viewed the Bible as compelling, irresistible truth, and as a precious treasure of infinite and divine wisdom. In yet another of its aspects, God's Word is seen as a dynamic, spiritual power.

Dr. J. Carl Laney, *professor of Biblical Literature at Western Seminary, points out that the same power and dynamism of the spoken word of God which created this world out of nothing is the power available in His Word today to change people's lives.*

THE WORD AS GOD'S UNIQUE DYNAMIC:
Its Spiritual Power

J. CARL LANEY

SUNKEN gold from wrecked Spanish galleons continues to lure treasure hunters to the shallow waters off the Florida Keys. The odds of finding a hoard of silver coins or gold bars are few and the risks of underwater recovery are great. But the prospect of finding instant riches drives searchers on.

Roger Miklos, treasure hunter for a large salvage company, has remarked, "By a very conservative estimate of the treasure still lost off the U.S. coast between North Carolina and Florida, there is enough to put one million dollars in the pocket of every man, woman and child living in New York City." Thoughts like this have led Mel Fisher to devote the last twenty-three years of his life to the recovery of sunken treasure. "Once you see the ocean bottom carpeted with gold coins, you'll never forget it," he says.[1]

On June 13, 1971, as he was scouring the ocean floor for clues, one of Mel's divers surfaced with nearly eight feet of exquisite gold chain from what turned out to be the legendary

Nuestra Senora de Atocha. As they continued to probe the sea bottom, they found silver and gold coins, gold bars, gold chains and rings—treasure worth an estimated six million dollars.

For the last fifteen years Mel has searched the sea floor around the wreck looking for the remaining treasure worth an estimated 100 million dollars. But the cost has been high in equipment, legal expenses, and human life. The search has already claimed four victims, including Mel's son and daughter-in-law.

As exciting as it would be to recover gold from a Spanish galleon, the Bible reveals that the truth of God's Word is a treasure of far greater value. The psalmist declared:

> The law of Thy mouth is better to me
> Than thousands of gold and silver pieces. (119:72)

> Therefore I love Thy commandments
> Above gold, yes above fine gold. (119:127)

The riches we enjoy from God's Word are eternal, offering the way of salvation and God's plan for abundant, fulfilling life.

We focus our attention in this study on the immeasurable value of the Bible as God's unique dynamic for spiritual life.

THE VITALITY OF GOD'S WORD—HEBREWS 4:12

The book of Hebrews was written to encourage Hebrew Christians to recognize that Christ has completed the work of redemption. No longer need they carry on the Jewish sacrificial system. In chapter 4 the writer exhorts these believers to cease their works and rest in Christ's finished work.

The instrument God uses to bring us into this faith-rest life is the Word of God which is introduced and described in verse 12. Here we discover that the Word is energetic in its operation. God's Word is described as "living." Although more than two thousand years old, God's Word contains no "dead" utterance of the past. The Bible contains God's "living oracles" (Acts 7:38), for the living God still speaks through this book.

It is a "living and abiding word" (1 Peter 1:23) because when it is planted in our hearts, it yields eternal life!

God's Word is also described as "active." It fulfills the purpose for which it has been uttered. As God declares in Isaiah 55:11, "My word which goes forth from My mouth . . . shall not return to Me empty, without accomplishing what I desire, and without succeeding in the matter for which I sent it." God's prophecies are always realized. His words never fail.

Hebrews 4:12 teaches that the Word is effective in its discrimination. The Word of God is compared to a sword sharpened on both edges so it can cut from both directions. As a sharp sword can penetrate bone and marrow, so God's Word can probe the innermost recesses of our spiritual being ("soul and spirit").

The phrase "able to judge" suggests the winnowing process so familiar to ancient farmers. In biblical times grain was threshed and then winnowed. The winnowing separated the chaff from the grain. The worthless, broken straw was burned. The kernels of grain were stored for later use. Similarly, God uses His Word to winnow our hearts and thoughts, separating that which is good and useful from that which has no place in our lives.

Often while reading the Word I have had a verse penetrate my heart and show me my neglect in a particular area. "Oops, I guess I am missing the mark here, Lord. Help me to get back on track by the power of the Holy Spirit."

Hebrews 4:12 reveals that God's Word is a unique and powerful dynamic for spiritual life. But you would probably like more specifics. D. L. Moody said, "God did not give us the Scriptures to increase our knowledge, but to change our lives." How can and does God's dynamic Word transform us?

THE POWER OF GOD'S WORD—PSALM 19:7-10

The power of the Bible to change lives is evidenced by the words of a South Sea islander during World War Two, who proudly displayed his New Testament to a G.I. "In America we have outgrown that sort of thing," the soldier responded. The native smiled back, "It's a good thing we haven't. If it wasn't for this Book, you'd have been a meal by now!"

Psalm 19 is an eloquent statement of the power of God's Word to change lives. The psalm presents two aspects of God's revelation—the revelation of His glory through creation (verses 1-6) and the revelation of His truth through the Law (7-14).

The *general* revelation of God in nature proclaims the majesty of the Creator, but is insufficient to significantly change our lives because it does not reveal Christ.

And so the psalmist shifts his praise to the *special* revelation of God through His Word. Here we discover what the transforming power of God's Word can accomplish.

The pattern David follows in this description of God's Word is to designate it with some appropriate adjective, and finally to associate it with some beneficial effect. In short, he tells us first what the Word "is" and then what it "does."

Restoring the Soul. The first synonym David uses to describe God's Word is the term "law," or *torah,* which literally means direction, teaching or instruction. The words, "of Yahweh," identify the one from whom this instruction comes. It comes from God—the covenant making God of Israel.

The law is described as "perfect." It is entirely in accord with truth. The Bible is a perfect revelation of God's instruction to man. This means that it is without error and completely reliable as a guide for faith and practice.

When God's instruction comes in contact with our lives it brings restoration. For the unbeliever, this "turning back" of the soul involves repentance and belief in Jesus Christ. This is the "renewing by the Holy Spirit" spoken of by Paul (Titus 3:5). For the believer, this restoration involves the spiritual refreshment that comes when we open the Book and find its truths bringing renewal to our lives.

I can tell when the time is approaching for another tuneup

on my car. The car doesn't start as well and doesn't run as smoothly. Then on a Saturday morning, I will change the spark plugs and time the engine. What a difference a tuneup makes! So too, we as believers must "tune up" our spiritual lives by regular reading of the Word of God. We will find our lives running more smoothly and will respond better under pressure.

Making Wise the Simple. The next synonym used for the Word of God is "testimony." It is derived from the word "to bear witness" and indicates that the Scriptures "bear witness" to God's truth. Like witnesses in a court of law, the Scriptures give ongoing "testimony" to what God is like and what He has done.

Here David describes the Word as being "confirmed." In other words, it is established and sure. The Bible is not going to tell us one thing today and something different tomorrow.

God's Word promises to make the simple or naive person spiritually wise. The Bible has much to say about wisdom—the practical use of knowledge. A most exciting truth is found in Ecclesiastes 10:10—"Wisdom has the advantage of giving success."

The Bible is really a book on successful living—getting along with God, with family, with friends, with employers. There are those who teach that you must "dress for success." I would suggest that you *read* for success—and the textbook is God's Word!

Rejoicing the Heart. The first synonym used for the Word of God in verse 8 is the word "precept." It refers to an order which God has given for man to obey.

The charges which God has given man to obey are "right." The word comes from a verb meaning "to be smooth or straight." This word reminds me of an incident which took place a few days after my arrival in Manila for six months of ministry at the Asian Theological Seminary. I was just learning how to negotiate my way around our shopping district when I found myself driving against the traffic. The street got narrower and narrower. There had been no sign, but I was going the wrong way on a one-way street. It took all my driving skill and patience to get to the next intersection and out of that mess.

Disobeying God's charges is like going the wrong way down a one-way street. Your route will be neither smooth nor straight!

The effect of God's Word when directing us along the smooth or right way is to cause the whole inner man to "rejoice." God's Word brings a deep sense of joy to the lives of those who study and obey it. This inner happiness, I believe, flows from a clear conscience. This is suggested by the words of David after his sin with Bathsheba where he prayed, "Restore to me the joy of Thy salvation" (Psalm 51:12). Sin had scarred David's conscience and taken away his joy. On the other hand, the inner man rejoices when God's Word is obeyed.

Enlightening the Eyes. The next synonym for the Scripture is "commandment." It is related to the Hebrew word meaning "to give an order," and refers to the sum of God's orders or imperatives.

Here the Word of God is described as "pure." The same word is used in the Song of Solomon to describe the sun (6:10). As the sun gives light and is completely devoid of darkness, so God's Word gives pure light without any deception or error.

Advertisements by dealers in precious metals often promise that their coins are 99.5 percent pure. That means there is some alloy in the metal. Part of the gold coin isn't gold! God's Word, however, contains no alloy. You can depend on it 100 percent.

The Word is described in Psalm 119:105 as a "lamp to my feet." Here also in Psalm 19 this imagery is used to illustrate how God's Word illuminates our mental and spiritual faculties.

The wife of one of my students recently had a slight stroke which resulted in the loss of vision in one eye. As we prayed for her recovery we saw the Lord answer in a remarkable way. Slowly but surely, the blind spot was reduced. Instead of darkness, she saw light! Once again she was able to drive, read, and finally teach. While rejoicing in the recovery of her sight, we realize how much more important it is that we receive *spiritual* light from God's Word!

The expression "the fear of the Lord" is not really a designation of the law itself, but views the law with reference to its purpose—to teach us how to fear God (Deuteronomy 17:19).

The Word is said to be "clean." This suggests that it is ethically pure—consistent with the character of its divine Author.

The Bible endures forever. It does not offer mere opinions which may lose their value with the passing of time. Unlike science textbooks, it doesn't need revision when new discoveries are made or theories corrected. As Isaiah declared, "The grass withers, the flower fades, but the word of our God stands forever" (Isaiah 40:8).

Upholding Truth to Justice. The final synonym for the Word of God appears in verse nine. The term "judgments" calls attention to the fact that God is both Lawgiver and Judge. He is the One who decides cases and passes sentences. The Bible contains God's decisions concerning the duties and obligations of man.

These divine decisions are said to be "true" and "righteous." You can rely on the Word of God because it is consistent with the character of its Author.

On January 22, 1973, the United States Supreme Court made a very significant decision known as *Roe vs. Wade.* The Court swept aside all state regulations limiting abortions, granting women an absolute right to abortion on demand during the first two trimesters of pregnancy, and the almost unqualified right to abortion during the final trimester. As Christians we have protested this decision. We feel that the court erred in this decision, which has opened the floodgates to abortion in this country.

How thankful we are that God, the Sovereign Judge, makes no such errors in the decisions he renders. He consistently upholds truth and justice. His judgments can be trusted and must be obeyed.

THE VALUE OF GOD'S WORD—PSALM 19:10-11

David's praise of the spiritual dynamic of God's Word to change lives concludes with an expression of the desirability and sweetness of the law. God's Word is compared with gold and with honey.

Gold, that most precious of glittering metals, is sought by miners, jewelers, and investors around the world. Recently the glitter and glory of that precious metal has dimmed, however, as its exchange value has fallen from $850 per ounce to around $350.

Honey, that most delicious of natural treats, is sought by sweet-tooths everywhere! How well I remember the honey-drenched, sugar-sprinkled *sopapias* served at our favorite Mexican restaurant in Dallas, Texas. As delicious as they were, such treats are a memory, for I've not found ones like them anywhere since.

David is saying that the most refined gold and the sweetest honey provide less joy and satisfaction than the delight that comes from studying and obeying God's Word!

But David wants us to be reminded that the Bible is not just a sweet book to read—it is a divine book to heed!

Like road signs—"Slow!" "Danger!" "Beware of Slides!" "Slippery Road!" "Yield!"—God's Word warns us of impending danger. To read God's Word and not heed its warnings would be as foolish as ignoring road signs when driving.

David concludes with a positive thrust. God's Word warns us of danger and promises reward for obedience. Jesus affirmed this principle on the night before His death when He told His disciples that it wasn't enough just to know the things He taught: "You are blessed if you do them" (John 13:17).

GOD'S WORD AND YOU

The Bible is a divine book which has the power to change your life! But don't expect it to hit you like a jolt of adrenalin each time you read it. There will be occasional "jolts" when you discover new truths or come to a new awareness of the application of some important principle. But the benefits of regular reading of God's Word is more like taking vitamins.

A person does not take vitamins because of any surge of new strength throughout the body every time they are swallowed. Rather, one takes vitamins because of their long-term benefits. Taken consistently, they will help over the long haul to resist disease and to promote better physical health.

So it is with God's Word. The Bible is God's unique dynamic for spiritual life. As we read and apply it, our spiritual lives will be strengthened and our walk with God enhanced.

William Graham Scroggie was a man of the Word. Son of a Scottish evangelist, Scroggie devoted his life to the study and teaching of the Bible. He was convinced that God's Word must have an important place in the lives of all Christians. This concern is highlighted in the preface of his last book, *The Unfolding Drama of Redemption*.

There he writes that Christians must know the Bible better than any other book. Then he adds, "The Bible is given to us that we might know God, and live the life of His plan for us."[2]

It was this kind of commitment to knowing God and obeying His word that energized Scroggie and made him so successful in his life and ministry.

May this be true for you as you study and obey the Bible—God's unique dynamic for spiritual life.

NOTES

1. *National Geographic,* June 1976, p. 789.

2. Graham Scroggie, *The Unfolding Drama of Redemption* (Zondervan, 1972), p. 17.

One of the most respected secular philosophers of our century, Mortimer Adler, has written a book entitled, How To Think about God. *Through sixteen chapters of exquisitely reasoned argument, Adler moves the reader toward an inescapable conclusion: God exists—a fact which no honest, competent thinker can logically deny.*

"He does exist, and more than that," says Adler. "This God that exists is sovereign, omnipotent, omniscient and He can do with us as He wills."

Then Adler brings us to the final chapter, which he calls "To the Chasm's Edge." Though the author doesn't specifically state it, one senses in the chapter an almost plaintive cry for someone to come alongside and lift him over the chasm. "What we cannot know about this God by rational thought is whether or not he cares at all about us." In Adler's argument He is discovered, but He is silent.

Dr. W. Robert Cook, *professor of Biblical and Systematic Theology at Western Seminary, declares otherwise. He reminds us that God has spoke, and the Bible is His Word to man about Himself.*

C H A P T E R   4

THE WORD AS A REVELATION OF GOD: Its Divine Focus

W. ROBERT COOK

GOD by His nature is spirit, unseen, unknown and ineffable. He is other than, apart from, or transcendent over all that is created and finite, for He alone is uncreated and infinite.

His creation, however, has fallen into sin. Evil now permeates the Creator's material and immaterial handiwork. Consequently, there is both an ontological and a moral barrier separating mankind from any meaningful knowledge or experience of God. Apart from some divinely initiated action to the contrary, the only revelation of God mankind can anticipate is JUDGMENT.

This is only a part of the story. God by His nature is also involved directly with His creation, seeable, knowable and sufficiently effable to provide for meaningful communication between Himself and His moral creation.

He not only exists as ultimate reality, but also as a personal moral being Who is capable of being known and purposes to be known.

As He created the human race He imaged Himself therein. In doing so He took the first step in the process of discovering Himself to mankind. As an all-knowing being He created those who could, in a creaturely way, *know* themselves, one another, and Himself. As a supremely loving being He created those who could, in a creaturely way, *love* themselves, their fellows, and Himself. As a sovereign and omnipotent being He created those who could, in a creaturely way, *make personal, social and spiritual choices*.

With these truths before us our dilemma is apparent. The high and lofty One Who inhabits eternity, Who is thrice holy and loves with an everlasting love, desires communion with those who are His image. But those who are His image are thrice sinful, and if they exercise love at all it is fickle and self-serving. Left to themselves and on their own, mankind has no interest in the divinely designed message or proffered fellowship.

Showing divine longsuffering and perseverance, however, God raised up, redeemed, and equipped prophets and apostles to speak and write His message to those who bear His twisted image. One of these, who shunned the wisdom of men as a means of restoring the broken communion between Creator and creature, wrote:

> We do, however, speak a message of wisdom among the mature, but not the wisdom of this age or of the rulers of this age, who are coming to nothing. No, we speak of God's secret wisdom, a wisdom that has been hidden and that God destined for our glory before time began. None of the rulers of this age understood it, for if they had, they would not have crucified the Lord of glory. However, as it is written:
>
> > "No eye has seen,
> >   no ear has heard,
> > no mind has conceived
> >   what God has prepared
> >   for those who love him"—

but God has revealed it to us by his Spirit.

The Spirit searches all things, even the deep things of God. For who among men knows the thoughts of a man except the man's spirit within him? In the same way, no one knows the thoughts of God except the Spirit of God. We have not received the spirit of the world but the Spirit who is from God, that we may understand what God has freely given us. This is what we speak, not in words taught us by human wisdom but in words taught by the Spirit, expressing spiritual truths in spiritual words. The man without the Spirit does not accept the things that come from the Spirit of God, for they are foolishness to him, and he cannot understand them, because they are spiritually discerned. The spiritual man makes judgments about all things, but he himself is not subject to any man's judgment:

"For who has known the mind of the Lord
    that he may instruct him?"?

But we have the mind of Christ. (1 Corinthians 2:6-16)

I would like to consider three major areas of truth from this passage that have bearing on divine revelation and its focus. These are: (1) the nature of divine revelation; (2) the subject/object construct of divine revelation; and (3) the aim of divine revelation.

THE NATURE OF DIVINE REVELATION

Paul's avoidance of the wisdom of men in this setting is not because he despised it or regarded it as invalid in the larger purposes of God. Rather, it was his concern that one's faith not rest on any less a foundation than the wisdom of God. Note with me some of the characteristics of this divine wisdom, identified by the apostle.

Striking Names of Revelation. We note, first, that it is called "revelation" (2:10). Paul speaks of the act of revealing

which implies the product *revelation*. To reveal literally means
to remove the *kalumma*, the veil or covering. Its antonym is
kalupto, to hide, cover or conceal; to remove from view. Thus
revelation (*apokalupsis*) means unveiling, disclosure, uncovering. The term brings several implications with it. It implies
that whatever needs to be revealed already exists and simply
needs uncovering. It further implies that without this action
the truth in question would not have been discovered, would
remain unknown.

Secondly, this revelation is called wisdom which, gener-
ally speaking, views practical skill in the use of knowledge.
Because his audience was so enamored with the wisdom of
men, Paul takes some pains to qualify the wisdom that is
revelation. It is of another age than this present one and of
another ruler than the present ones. Presumably then, it is the
wisdom of the Sovereign of an eternal kingdom—permanent
and lasting rather than faddish and transient. Also, it is a secret,
hidden wisdom as far as the rulers of this age are concerned.
It predates and transcends time. It enables correct assessment
of eternal verities; specifically, it enables one to recognize and
acknowledge the Lord of glory.

The Rationality of Divine Revelation. That the Word is
rational is reinforced in at least three ways in this passage.

First of all, it is taught that divine revelation is *knowable/
understandable*. Paul draws an unmistakable connection between the Spirit Who knows the thoughts of God and the people
of God who have received that same Spirit in order that they
may know what God has given them (2:11-12).

In addition, divine revelation is *receivable*. Although the
unbeliever does not accept the things that come from the Spirit
(the thoughts of God), the implication is that the believer (the
spiritual person of verse 15) does accept them (verse 14).

Finally, divine revelation is seen to be rational in content
in that it is *tangible*. The thoughts of God known by the Spirit
of God, understood and received by the man/woman of God,

were spoken in Spirit-taught words (verse 13). Words have specific form and meaning designed to be understood and to convey truth. These spoken words are written in this text (and in this entire letter) to the Corinthians. Thus the logical, rational tangibility of the God-originated message is empirically verifiable through the exercise of both sight and sound, as well as spiritually verifiable through the witness of the Spirit.

The Personal Character of Revelation. The last thing we must note about the nature of revelation is that it is an action that takes place between persons (verse 10). It originates with a personal God ("God revealed") and is directed to human beings ("to us"). The personal quality of this revelation is further highlighted by the phrase that qualifies "us"; it is not just any person to whom God reveals things—it is "to those who love him" (verse 9).

THE SUBJECT/OBJECT CONSTRUCT OF DIVINE REVELATION

Since we have dealt first with the nature of divine revelation as set forth by Paul in this passage, the context for this next point is very naturally provided. The questions we must now answer are: Who does the revealing? What (who) is revealed? To whom is it (are they) revealed? Of necessity we must backtrack and cover some of the same ground from a slightly different vantage point.

The Divine Agent of Revelation. The subject of revelation, the revealer, is very plainly identified in the text (verses 7,10): It is God. But, does this refer to the entire Godhead or one of the persons thereof? It would seem that this must be a reference to the Father in light of the distinction drawn in verse 8 with the Lord Jesus and in verse 10 with the Holy Spirit.

The agent of revelation is also specified clearly. It is the Spirit of God (verses 10-12). On the basis of shared (intra-Godhead) information, revelation comes to us through the Spirit from the Father.

The Direct Object of Revelation. Grammatically, no object for the verb "revealed" is stated in verse 10. This is understandable because in the surrounding context the stuff of revelation is seen to be a complex of things. Ideologically, Paul identifies at least four aspects of what is revealed.

It is first of all God's secret wisdom (verse 7) as set forth in the gospel and embodied in Jesus Christ (1:30, cf. 1:24). Second, it is things God prepared, which He kept in readiness (2:9), things which He foreordained for our glory before time began (2:7). Third, it may be described as "the depths of God" (2:10; cf. Romans 11:33).

These are the things it is said the Spirit "searches." As the context clarifies, it is not that the Spirit is looking for information hitherto not available to Him, but rather that He is plumbing the depths (or as Arndt and Gingrich suggest, he "fathoms everything"; *A Greek-English Lexicon of the New Testament,* p. 306) of God for the believer's benefit.

What does the Spirit make known to us? Perhaps Romans 11:33 provides a clue to the answer. "O the depth of the riches both of the wisdom and knowledge of God! How unsearchable His judgments and untraceable His ways!" Godet suggests that the depths of God refers to "God's essence, then His attributes, volitions and plans" (*Commentary on St. Paul's First Epistle to the Corinthians,* I, 148). Charles Hodge understands it to describe "the inmost recesses . . . of his being, perfections, and purposes" (*An Exposition of the First Epistle to the Corinthians,* p. 39). These comments are right on target.

Verse 11 seems to continue the idea of verse 10, although most modern translations shift the emphasis just a little by what may be a too interpretive translation. In verse 10 the apostle speaks of *ta bathe tou Theou* (the depths of God) and in verse eleven he continues by referring to the fact that the Spirit of God knows *ta tou Theou* (the . . . of God). The ellipsis implies something important which is another aspect of the object of revelation. In keeping with the movement of Paul's argument here, it appears he refers to the "depths" of God in this passage. As no one among men knows the depths of a man's heart except the man himself, so no one knows the depths of God except the Spirit of God. And, we have received that Spirit.

Verse 12 tells the fourth aspect of what is revealed. The "what" of revelation is here described as "things freely given us by God." The sense of the word used here is that of a graciously given favor as opposed to the discharging of an obligation.

These aspects cumulate with significant impact. Since God's wisdom, knowledge, judgments, ways and grace are the object of revelation, we may rightly say God Himself is the object of revelation.

The Indirect Object of Revelation. As noted previously, those who love God are the intended recipients of revelation. Paul gives further specificity to this group by identifying them as the mature (verse 6), and by contrasting them with the rulers of this age and the natural man (verses 6,14). Those who love God are identified in Romans 8:28 as "the called according to [God's] purpose." In this context the mature are identified with those who may be designated as "spiritual" and "have the mind of Christ" (1 Corinthians 2:15-16) as over against those who are "of flesh" and "babes in Christ" (3:1).

THE AIM OF DIVINE REVELATION

Finally, we must give brief attention to the aim or intended outcome of divine revelation. What did God have in mind in disclosing what He has about Himself? A more complete study of our subject would certainly give a more extended answer to this question than will be offered here. This passage, however, does give some very basic and enlightening answers.

Internal Aim. In verse 14, Paul uses the device of instruction by contrast to identify three things about his intentions for revelation. (1) Whereas the natural (unbelieving) man does not accept the things of the Spirit of God (in this context, revelation, at the very least), they are by design intended to be accepted. The verb "accept" has in view an active "welcome," not a passive receiving. God's aim involves attitude as well as action. (2) The natural man, on the one hand, examines and assesses these things as foolishness (stupidity, silliness), whereas in reality they are genuine wisdom (cf. 3:19). (3) Although the natural man does not have the ability to understand them, these things are intended to be and may be understood by those who have received the Spirit (see 2:12).

Thus, the internal aim of divine revelation is that it be rightly received, rightly assessed and rightly understood.

External Aim. In contrast to the unbelieving person who rejects revelation, the spiritual person is enabled by revelation to examine all things. Revelation becomes the divine criterion by which to evaluate all of reality. It does not provide one with all possible information about all things. Rather, it provides a standard against which to measure the value of any and all things.

Christological Aim. The question Paul quotes from Isaiah 40:13 is a rhetorical one: "For who has known the mind of the Lord, that he should instruct Him?" The expected answer is: No one. And yet, the apostle surprises us by saying, in essence, *we have* God's mind (although he does not go on to conclude that we therefore instruct Him). Because we have divine revelation, "we have the mind of Christ." We may view things as Christ does. This means that our fellowship with Him will be enhanced because of commonly shared outlooks on things, and that our general perception of life will be more in keeping with things as they really are.

The Practical Aim. We have reviewed together a familiar passage and what it has to say to us about divine revelation. What difference does it make?

Perhaps the significance of these truths can be illustrated by another question. Ask yourself what things would be like if God had chosen to withhold any revelation of Himself. Not only would we be ignorant about the God of reality, but we would know very little about ourselves and our world. We would have a desire and perhaps even a sense of need for ultimate truth, but would have no way of attaining it. We would be ever seeking and never finding. Our beliefs would be based upon the imaginations of fallen men, but we would have no standard by which to measure their error. We would be those creatures of God with the greatest potential, yet with no way to realize it. We could cry out in desperate need and be heard by God, but would be left in the deafening silence of a universe rushing madly toward perdition with no word of response.

As we contemplate these things we should be moved to pray: Thank You, Father, that You have unveiled Yourself to us in deed and word and in the person of Your Son! Thank You for the unfathomable grace that has moved You to make Yourself known to us at an intimate level! In the name of Jesus Christ our Lord, Amen.

Recently Harvard University celebrated its 350th birthday. A notable thing about that venerable campus is the ubiquitous university motto. You see it everywhere—engraved on the facades of the old stone buildings, carved deep in arches of gates and doorways, emblazoned on banners in the old halls. It even appears as the logo on letterheads and bookcovers. Veritas. Truth. What a fine and noble motto for an institution of learning.

In its earliest days it was the symbol of what a godly faculty sought to declare and instill in its students—it rested soundly on a conviction straight from Scripture. A hundred years later, in the secular drift, it had become less a declaration and more a search. In the modern era it finds its expression in a question: What is truth?

***Dr. Gerry Breshears,** assistant professor of Systematic Theology at Western Seminary, explains that the Bible is our revelation from God, teaching us that truth and life are inseparable. He leads us to examine the life-imparting nature of the God-given Word, the Word as spiritual seed.*

CHAPTER 5

THE WORD AS SPIRITUAL SEED:
Its Life-giving Purpose

GERRY BRESHEARS

IN five evenings of TV and a book, Phil Donahue has examined the human animal. Donahue, described as "TV's leading example of a sensitive, highly evolved male primate,"[1] asked three basic questions about humans: "Who are we?" "Why do we act the way we do?" "Can we change?"

THE HUMAN ANIMAL

"Who are we?" According to Donahue we are animals who have evolved to be human. We have not ceased to be animal. That nature endures even in the highest stage of evolution. Our primitive animal nature gives us the powerful passions which control us. Our evolved humanness gives us the power and the drive to continue our evolutionary trek.

Love and sex define the human animal, according to Donahue. Sex demonstrates our animal heritage, exposing our deepest passions. Love discloses our humanness, shown in caring for another. Understand the tension between these two and you have the key to understanding the human animal.

Why do we act the way we do? Because of the combination of genetic nature and cultural nurture which configures us as individuals. Nature deals the cards. Nurture teaches us how to play them. Nature gives us the sexual passion and a deep human need for love. Cultural nurture provides a very imperfect awareness of our nature and an even less perfect adeptness in meetings our needs.

Think again of the basic human attributes: love and sex. There is a breach between these two because our culture nurtures us improperly. The breach brings such dilemmas as teenage pregnancy, divorce, and great dissatisfaction in life. Donahue reports that the failure is so serious that less than half of us *ever* succeed at uniting love and sex. The reason for the failure lies with poor education, i.e., deficient nurture.

Can we change? Only if we understand ourselves as human animals and dedicate ourselves to doing a better job. Only if our nurturing improves.

What of the tragedies flowing from the breach between sex and marriage? How would Donahue solve the problems of teenage pregnancy, for example? Abstinence outside of marriage does not even merit consideration. It does not give proper weight to our animal nature, apparently. The ideal of monogamy, faithfulness in marriage, merits only scorn. It can't be translated into the workaday reality, he asserts.[2] What is *his* solution? More sex education and dispensing birth control materials in the high schools. How this will unite love and sex escapes me.

What of the violence which plagues our American civilization at every level, invading every aspect of our lives, causing us to think every problem best solved with a gun, a blow, a razorlike word? He observed that animals almost never kill or seriously injure other members of their own species. Why do human animals hurt each other so often? Donahue asserts that the problem rises out of private property which leads to greed, selfishness, and the desire to steal and to hurt. Civilization with its rules of property is the cause of violence. His romantic notion of charging civilization with the blame for our violence suggests that the solution is to become more natural, i.e., more like animals. Proper nurture will make us more natural.

Such "solutions" expose the bankruptcy of the series and the world view it promotes.

THE CREATED HUMAN

Christians must answer these same questions. Even more importantly, we must answer them for a world which reckons Phil Donahue and his spiritual kin saviors of the human animal.

Who are we? Persons created in God's image,[3] persons with rationality, self-consciousness, volition, self-identity, permanence, moral capacity,[4] emotion, and, above all, persons whose identity finally depends on relationship with God.

Why do we act the way we do? Why do sinful thoughts and behavior erupt so regularly from persons created in God's image? Because the sin nature is endemic to humanity. This nature, flowing from its Adamic source, pervades our humanness extenively and intensively. Every aspect of every person reaps the result of Edenic sin. We personally ratify this nature with every thought and with every deed. The enigma of human perversity which puzzles philosopher and psychologist finds its solution in the doctrine of original sin.

Can we change? Only if we are sinful. This sounds like a hopeless contradiction, but it is true. Sinfulness flows from misused moral capacity. That same moral capacity, when renewed by the gracious work of God, is the basis for true moral change in the individual. Humans can be sinful only if they are created in the image of God, created for relationship with God with the capabilities of rational self-transcendence, moral self-determination and personal relationship. The image makes us responsible agents who can obey. It also makes us able to disobey responsibility, which is to sin.

All the other "explanations" of human perversity,[5] including Donahue's, either elevate humans to divinity or reduce them to animals. The former explanation leaves humans to solve their own problems. The latter leaves no solution except to cope with our animalness. Only defining humans as sinners who yet retain the image of God adequately explains who we are and why we act as we do.

THE LIFE-GIVING WORD

This brings us to the purpose of God's revelation in His life-giving Word. He comes to us in order to renew sinful humans by the life-giving power of His living Word. He graciously renews us in His image when He regenerates us (Titus 3:5), giving us a new heart of obedience (Romans 6:17; 2 Corinthians 3:3) in which the capacities of the image once again become instruments of righteousness (Romans 6:13).

His promises are clear: "As the rain and snow come down from heaven, and do not return to it without watering the earth and making it bud and flourish, so that it yields seed for the sower and bread for the eater, so is My word that goes out from My mouth; It will not return to Me empty, but will accomplish what I desire and achieve the purpose for which I sent it" (Isaiah 55:11). When Jesus tells the parable of the soils, He explains that the seed which brings life and fruitfulness is the Word of God (Luke 8:11). Peter tells us, "You have been born again, not of perishable seed, but of imperishable, through the living and enduring Word of God" (1 Peter 1:23).

God's Word is a unique, imperishable seed, implanted in our hearts by God as a spiritual seed, overcoming sin's devastation, renewing every aspect of our person. As the Spirit works through God's Word, we become human, persons recreated in the image of God.

A full exploration of the life-giving power of God's Word would take us to every aspect of the image of God, to every element of personality, to rationality, self-consciousness, volition, self-identity, permanence, moral capacity. For now, we will give our attention to just one of the areas where the living Word of God does its renewing work. We will look at our mind, the rational capacity of the image of God. We will see how the Word gives information we lack, power to overcome sin's devastation, and how its living character applies these to our minds.

"Mind" describes more the content and direction of our thinking than the process of thinking itself.[6] The unrenewed mind will be directed toward things which are merely human, merely earthly. The mind renewed by the Word will live with eternity's values in view. *Mind* speaks to the fundamental assumptions, values, allegiances by which one lives. Paul in Romans 8:5-7 teaches us that *mind* expresses not only the activity of the intellect, but the direction of life, the movement of the will.

We must understand that the Word enlivens our minds, enabling a Spirit-renewed thought life, one which centers on the foundational knowledge of God, one which centers its values and allegiances according to Him and views all of life with the mind of Christ.

THE WORD'S LIFE-GIVING INFORMATION

I always loved airplanes. As a boy I dreamed of flying airliners packed with people. The onset of nearsightedness ended the dream at age twelve, but not the love of airplanes. That love brings on a terrible fascination when air travel becomes air tragedy. It brought me to the crash site of one airplane in the early morning hours after its midnight crash. I saw the broken remains of the intricate flying machine strewn among the trees just below the crest of a mountain. I looked at the structural materials inside the wing with feelings like those upon seeing the bone and blood vessels of a shattered human. The pilot had been flying home after a routine training mission. There was no hint of trouble until he smashed into the mountain top. He misread his altimeter . . . a fatal mistake.

Donahue shows me that people are like the pilot of that plane. They misread the "instrument panels" of their lives. They do not know the right thing to do. That the Bible shows us what is best for our lives never seriously enters their minds. For example, uniting love and sex in a marriage which is a publicly pledged, permanent, exclusive, heterosexual union [7] is an idealistic myth, not a realistic option for "modern America." Examples of the value of such a union abound, but the information is not transmitted from the "instrument panel" to the mind of unrenewed people.

Paul explains that when people block out God's revelation, "their foolish hearts are darkened. Professing to be wise, they became fools" (Romans 1:21-22).

The Word of God enlightens our minds, helping us see God's "instrument panel." With the illumination of the Spirit we not only perceive the instruments but interpret the significance of their readings for our lives. The living Word enables us to understand our world, our place in the world, the reality of depravity, and God's solution for the problem. It helps us comprehend these by placing them against the presupposition of God.

The Word shows us that goodness must be defined in terms of godliness, humanness in terms of the image of God, sanity in terms of humility before God and worship of God. Because the secular mind rejects this information, it will never satisfactorily answer Donahue's three questions.

THE WORD'S LIFE-GIVING POWER

The problem with our minds goes beyond a lack of information. Many who have the right information cannot pattern their lives according to the truth. The mind is more than information. It includes values and allegiances as well.

My love of flying made me all the more sensitive to a gripping recording in one of the old Moody Institute of Science films. A novice pilot, overtaken by bad weather, found himself literally fighting for his life.

A cloud surrounded him. Suddenly he was utterly disoriented. He cried into his radio for help. The controller directed the pilot's attention to the proper instruments. The terrified pilot could read them, but could not follow their directions. The controller tried to tell him how to move the controls. The panic-stricken pilot could not. Finally, in desperation the controller begged the pilot to release the controls in hope that the aircraft would right itself. The only sound: "Help!. . . Help!"

This pilot fully realized his trouble. He knew the imminency of death. He cried for help. But when help came, he had not the power to utilize it. Life-saving information came to him, but his panic-clouded mind could not translate that information, precious as it was, into life-saving action.

Think back to Donahue's third question, "Can we change?" His prescription for changing the way we act is education. He contends that sex education will solve the breach between love and sex, that drug education will end the tragedy of addiction, that nurture in gentleness will end the horror of violence. He continues to promote these solutions despite their long history of failure. He fails to realize the cloud of sin that darkens our minds. Like the pilot lost in the clouds, humans cannot process even the best of information, cannot turn it into lifesaving action. Spiritual truth without the spiritual power gives no spiritual life (1 Corinthians 2:14).

The Bible tells us the root of our dilemma springs from Adam (Romans 5:12-21; 1 Corinthians 15:21-22)—hardly a popular or easy answer! Pascal put it this way, "Certainly nothing jolts us more rudely than this doctrine, and yet for the mystery, the most incomprehensible of all, we remain incomprehensible to ourselves."[8] Difficult as the doctrine may be, without it we can neither understand nor change ourselves.

Donahue's solution fails because it has no answer for the depraved nature we inherit from Adam. Because he and his kin reject God's assessment of the human problem, their diagnosis of the human malady is tragically wrong. Their attempts to solve the human predicament will be as hopeless as trying to cure pneumonia with blood-letting, as deadly as treating a cancerous growth with Dr. Scholl's corn pads, as fatal as a novice flying inside a cloud.

Let's look at an example of how the Word renews our mind. The Word tells us to be holy by transforming our minds (Romans 12:2). One way to do this is to fill our minds with what is true, noble, right, pure, lovely, admirable, excellent and praiseworthy (Philippians 4:8). As we think in our hearts, so are we (Proverbs 23:7). The Word powerfully gives life when we fill ourselves with it.

Contrast the mind of the human animal as presented on TV. It teaches us to love things, to love ecstatic sensations, to love independence. It tells us to measure success by how many things you gather to yourself, reminding us that you can have it all. It tells us to seek heightened sexual stimulation, that a certain beer can make the night the best part of the day. It tells us to seek total independence, to master the possibilities, to have it your way. These messages are not naive. They are outright deceptions, designed to appeal to human animals. Judging from the changes in the last few years, "you can bet your Nielsen rating it will get worse."[9]

What we fill our minds with directly affects our behavior. Proverbs 23:7 is richly confirmed by all manner of studies. For example, these studies link watching violence with violent behavior. A few years ago Ronald Zamora, 14, shot and killed an 82-year-old widow. His defense was that he was just acting out a TV script. Acting under the influence of prolonged, intense, involuntary subliminal television violence, "pulling the trigger became as common to him as killing a fly."[10] The incident was eerily similar to two television episodes the boy had recently watched. Although his attempt to shift blame to TV was rejected, no one denied the impact of his steady diet of violence.

The connection between what we fill our minds with and what we do is applied inconsistently at best. We are led to believe that viewing sexually explicit scenes has no effect on sexual behavior. Although it correlates immediately with viewing violence leading to violent behavior, the seemingly obvious notion that viewing sexual immorality on TV, movies, music videos, and magazines will lead to sexually immoral behavior is rejected out of hand. Violence breeds violence, but sexual immorality is immensely profitable.

As our minds absorb the content of God's powerful Word, they will increasingly conform to Christ's. Our lives will change to conform to His. The change comes because of the power which resides in the Word itself.

THE LIVING WORD

When we receive the Spirit of God at our new birth, He mediates the Word to our hearts. The Word is much more than a book of information. The Bible is a living book by virtue of the living Spirit's working.

I am a computer hobbyist . . . a guru to my friends. One morning I came back from a breakfast with some students to find my friend literally screaming mad. On my advice he had purchased a powerful computer with the most powerful software available. He had stacks of manuals with every conceivable bit of information about his computer and its software. When he fired up the machine, he had received an error message. For an hour and more he sought to tap the power of his computer, but the same error message frustrated every attempt. He searched his pile of manuals for the answer to the problem. The disarray in his office graphically demonstrated how hard he tried. The ever recurring error message mutely confirmed the inadequacy of the manuals, the barrenness of mere power.

I walked into his office. After a passing glance at the monitor, I tapped two keys. The error message vanished. The machine's power awaited his request.

My friend had no shortage of power, no inadequacy of information. But without personal help, no solution was to be found. He needed a living person who knew the machine, who could analyze his situation and relate the vast amount of information to his problem. More information, more power, would only compound his problem. He needed a living person, a helper, a paraclete to enable him to utilize the information and power he already had.

Although all persons can understand the powerful facts of the Bible with sufficient study, only the Holy Spirit can help us move from impersonal facts to know the personal significance of the facts, the certainty that here is the voice of God speaking directly to me (1 Corinthians 10-14). White Heart's catchy song title puts it neatly: the living Word enables us to "Walk that Talk." The Spirit who makes the Bible a living book enables us to translate that content of knowledge into living by the renewing of hearts and minds. Only He, through God's Word, is able to transform our sin-darkened minds with life-giving power.

THE CHALLENGE TO PRODUCE LIFE

In the preface to the Great Bible of 1540, Archbishop Cranmer wrote:

> In the Scripture be the fat pastures of the soul; therein is no venomous meat, no unwholesome thing; they be very dainty and pure feeding. He that is ignorant, shall find there what he should learn . . . Here may all manner of persons, men, women, young, old, learned, unlearned, rich, poor, priests, laymen, lords, ladies, officers,

> tenants, and mean men, virgins, wives, widows, lawyers,
> merchants, artificers, husbandmen, and all manner of
> persons, of what estate or condition so ever they be, may
> in this book learn all things what they ought to believe,
> what they ought to do, and what they should not do, as
> well concerning Almighty God, as also concerning
> themselves and all other.[11]

The Word tells us to "crave the pure spiritual milk, so that *by it* you may grow up in your salvation" (1 Peter 2:1-2). The Spirit does not work apart from the Word, and the Word is merely academic without the Spirit. Together they become the living Word of God which produces life as we fill our minds with it. It enlivens our minds, giving us the proper foundations for understanding, ordering our priorities, values and allegiances, guiding our conduct, freeing our wills so that we become fulfilled as humans, instruments of God's glory. As we comprehend the great themes and principles of Scripture, we will comprehend the world and ourselves because we know our creation, sin, redemption and purpose from God's vantage point.

This is the charge I bring to you: Know the life-giving power of the Word. Know its purpose and power for renewing sinful humans, sinner and saint alike. Without it, we would be condemned to the mind of the human animal. With the living Word, we become instruments of renewal in a world dominated by the mind of the human animal. With it, we become conformed to the standards, values, allegiances, and goals of the living God.

NOTES

1. Joanne Ostrow, "TV Week," *Denver Post,* August 19, 1986, p. 5.
2. His guest argued that until recently the average marriage was only a dozen or so years due to death in childbirth, accidents, disease, and the like. However, this overlooks the obvious fact that many marriages lasted

much longer and that the expectation for all marriages was a lifelong commitment. Then, as now, love should precede sex. The courting procedures develop the love relationship which gives the context for a truly fulfilling sexual relationship.

3. Anthony Hoekema in *Created in God's Image* (Grand Rapids: Eerdmans, 1986) has a very fine discussion of the image of God. He sees it in two aspects: *structural*, which includes the endowment of gifts and capacities that enable man to function as he should in his various relationships and callings; and *functional*, which means man's proper functioning in harmony with God's will for him. My understanding is very similar.

4. Henry Stob, *Theological Reflections* (Grand Rapids: Eerdmans, 1981), pp. 56-57.

5. Bernard Ramm, *Offense to Reason* (San Francisco: Harper & Row, 1985), pp. 10-37, asks, "If Adam didn't, who did?" His survey of options, although very brief, helps one see the range of attempts to avoid an Adamic source as well as their failures.

6. J. Goetzmann, "Mind," in *New International Dictionary of New Testament Theology,* Colin Brown, ed. (Grand Rapids: Zondervan, 1976), II: 616-620. The classic work is Henry Blamires, *The Christian Mind* (Ann Arbor: Servant Books, 1978).

7. John Stott, *Involvement* (Old Tappan, N.J.: Fleming H. Revell, 1984), p. 66.

8. Blaise Pascal, *Pensees,* #131. Quoted by Ramm, p.1.

9. John MacArthur, *Why Believe the Bible* (Glendale, Calif.: Regal Books, 1980), p. 78.

10. *Time,* October 10, 1977, p. 87.

11. Quoted by J. I. Packer, *God Speaks to Man* (Philadelphia: Westminster Press, 1965), p. 86.

There is a vivid and permanent image etched in my mind, a haunting and remembered photograph. It was taken by a war correspondent; it was 1945, Buchenwald, and the photo was of a fence. However, it is not the fence so much that remains deeply engraved in my mind, but the dozens of bony fingers reaching through it, fingers attached to skeletons. The amazing thing about the skeletons is that they were alive. Bone, only bone, with skin stretched agonizingly over it, but alive.

Those skeletons remain forever with us, as they should. What the mind rejects is that the human body should look like that. It ought to have flesh and muscle, and there ought to be life and energy coursing through veins and arteries. But these Buchenwald captives were reduced to nothing but bone and skin.

When I get past the wretchedness of their condition, the thing most striking is the look on the faces. The look. Where one might expect some distorted and twisted look of pain and agony, a crying out in protestation about such a condition of the body, there is none. Almost uniformly across the photograph the look on the faces is empty, vacant, distant—the look of resignation. It is as if those poor souls had somehow reached the perverse conclusion that their condition was normal and to be expected.

What would it be like if our spiritual condition were as visible on the outside as our physical condition? What would be the look on our faces? Would there be the look of protest at the terrible spiritual condition some might be in? Or would there have settled in a look of resignation that somehow things were as they should be?

Convinced that the body needs nutrition, so even more should we be convinced that the soul and spirit need spiritual food. **Dr. J. Grant Howard,** *professor of Pastoral Theology at Western Seminary, shows us the Word as that spiritual food, life-giving and life-sustaining.*

C H A P T E R   6

THE WORD AS SPIRITUAL FOOD:
Its Life-building Purpose

J. GRANT HOWARD

THE Word of God is clearly linked to growth in 1 Peter 2:2.

Like newborn babes, long for the pure milk of the Word,
that by it you may grow in respect to salvation.

Here the believer is likened to a newborn baby, and the Word is likened to pure milk. As the baby longs for milk that will cause physical growth, so the believer is to long for the Word which will cause spiritual growth.

We are quite familiar with this phenomenon of growth in the physical realm. When we drink a glass of milk and eat a raw carrot (solid food), these substances go into our stomachs and are absorbed and distributed throughout our entire bodies, maintaining health and promoting growth. Milk and solid food contain the nutrients we need to nourish every cell in our bodies. I don't fully understand how all this works, but I do know that to stay alive and to remain healthy and to grow I must regularly ingest liquid and solid foods. That which I ingest, my body will digest.

How, we ask, does this work in the spiritual realm? The Word is like milk, but we certainly don't drink it. The Word is like solid food, but we certainly don't chew it up and swallow it. Nor do we have access to some kind of a "biblical blender" into which we can put the milk and solid food of the Word of God, whip it into a rich, creamy "sanctified shake" and swig it down.

If we don't ingest it by literally drinking and eating it, how do we take it in? With our ears we listen to it. With our eyes we read it. With our minds we observe it, probe it, study it, seek to understand it, memorize it, and store it. With our will we decide what needs to be done and we do it. God has given each believer all the receiving equipment he or she needs to take His Word into their life. In addition, the Holy Spirit indwells each believer as a resident teacher, prompting us toward the truth, protecting us from error (John 14:26; 1 John 2:20; 1 Corinthians 2:10-16). Even though the Spirit and the Word are separate entities, it is clear that they always work together, for the "sword of the Spirit . . . is the word of God" (Ephesians 6:17). So, we know that we *can* take the Word into our lives, but how do we know if we *are* taking it in? What evidence will prove that we are not only ingesting it but also digesting it? What signs do we look for that will prove we are feeding on the Word? First Peter 2:2 tells us that we ought to grow—but without telling us how to evaluate whether we are growing.

THE EVIDENCE OF GROWTH

Is the evidence an occasional biblical burp, designed to prove we have been feasting on the heavenly manna? Do we get spiritually heavier—weighing in each Sunday to see how much we have gained? Do we demonstrate it by regularly raising our spiritual IQ? Are we able to bench-press more commentaries? Do we run some kind of spiritual marathon, seeking to lower our time each race? Or is it a spiritual triathlon or pentathlon or even a decathlon where we are seeking to outlast and outscore everyone else—demonstrating our spiritual prowess in various evangelical events?

Is the evidence of our spiritual diet the amount of Scripture we have read? Memorized? Studied? Exegeted? Taught? Preached? Perhaps it is shown by the number of courses we have taken—and passed—with an "A."

If it's none of the above, and obviously it isn't, then what are the marks of a growing Christian? We can find at least five things to look for:

(1) *Believing* is the first identifying factor. When we are learning to live dependently trusting, we are growing.

(2) When we are increasing in our *knowledge* of God, we are growing.

(3) When we are *obeying* the commands of God, this too is evidence of personal growth.

(4) If we are *changing*, becoming more like Christ, this is further proof of our progress.

But I said there were five things to look for and I have mentioned only four. The fifth one is *discerning*. It too is basic, but probably not as frequently developed. We consistently refer to the importance of knowing and doing, and rightly so. Discerning is the bridge that links knowing and doing. Let's explore this significant aspect of growth.

THE PLACE OF DISCERNMENT

The Biblical Terms for Discernment. One of the main words in the Greek New Testament that connotes discernment is the root verb *krino* and its compound *anakrino*, *diakrino*, and *katakrino*. These words were used in courtroom situations to describe the judicial process of sifting through evidence to

determine what is right and what is wrong. One who did that
had to have discernment, i.e., had to be a very discerning
person. The other primary word for discernment is *dokimazo*.
This term conveys the idea of testing something, like ore, to
determine if it is genuine and pure. The testing process, often
carried out with chemicals or heat, is still one that is designed
to discern the true nature of the substance, whether it is valid
or invalid.

Both of the above words are translated similarly with
words like assess, appraise, examine, prove, judge, decide,
investigate, and test. "Discern" is a word which seems to
adequately and accurately capture the meaning of the other
terms. It literally means "to distinguish between."

The Biblical Message. Christians are to *examine the Word*
in order to determine its meaning. "He that is spiritual" says
Paul, "appraises all things." In the context, "all things" is seen
to refer to the truths that God has chosen to reveal to us by
His Spirit in the Word. The Bereans applied themselves similarly, "examining the Scriptures daily, to see whether these
things were so" (Acts 17:11). Paul challenges Timothy to *accurately handle* the word of truth (2 Timothy 2:15). So we see
that our God-given powers of discernment are first and foremost
to be directed toward an understanding of the Word. The clear
implication is that any believer can do this.

Christians are then able to *examine themselves:* to test
their spiritual position, i.e., to make sure they are in the faith
(2 Corinthians 13:5); and to test their lifestyle, to see if they
are walking worthy (1 Corinthians 11:27-28).

Thirdly, Christians are also to *examine the world* in which
they live. Listen to the words of Paul: "Examine everything
carefully, hold fast to that which is good; abstain from every
form of evil" (1 Thessalonians 5:21-22). The sensitive believer
is able to pause and test each life situation and determine the
right attitude to have and the right action to engage in.

The Basic Meaning of Discernment. Our ability to discern
the Word and ourselves readies us to competently discern the

problems and possibilities in our world. Discernment is the crucial link between knowing and doing. It is relating the truth we know to the life we live. It could be compared to what happens in a football game during the huddle. Based on the score, time left in the game, position on the field, the offensive team he has with him, the defense he is up against, input from coaches on the sidelines and spotters in the press box, and numerous other factors, the quarterback *discerns* which play should be run next. He calls it; the team performs it; and back into the huddle they go for more discernment. Sometimes the quarterback calls time out and goes to the sideline to get all the help he can from his discerning coaches. On occasion, the believer needs to seek added wisdom from veterans with seasoned discernment.

Discernment, then, is a critical component of one's Christian life. It takes life out of the realm of the mechanical and puts it into the realm of the decisional. Discernment goes beyond mere knowledge and leads us into proper action, but is a significant step in itself that is distinct from both knowledge and action. A person may *know and not do*. That is an intellectualized Christianity. A person may *do and not know*. That is an activist Christianity. But when knowing and doing are functioning properly, discernment can and must be taking place.

We may liken this process to a restaurant experience. There are two basic functions—ordering and eating—plus one other significant function—cooking. The menu is mandatory. You need to know what your eating options are. But you don't eat the menu! Eating is also mandatory. You have to assimilate the food into your body if it is going to do you any good. But you don't eat the plates, silverware, glasses, and napkins! Between ordering and eating there must be preparing, cooking, and serving. The kitchen experience links the ordering and eating. If we are to live and grow, we must have all three. A kitchen without orders is of no value. Orders without a kitchen are just as useless. Eating without a kitchen is impossible. A valid restaurant experience necessitates all three—ordering, cooking, and eating. A valid spiritual experience also necessitates a mandatory threesome—knowing, discerning, and doing. These three phases are developed by Paul in Romans 12.

THE MANIFESTATION OF DISCERNMENT

The message of Romans 12:1-2 can be outlined with several key words:

Presentation. The thrust of verse 1 is for the believer to make himself available to God for service. It is a responsibility placed upon every Christian. Based on what God has done for us, there comes the appeal from God to present ourselves as living sacrifices for Him.

Program (verse 2a). Having given ourselves to God, we are immediately enrolled in a program of growth and change that involves both negative and positive factors. The negative factor is to *stop being conformed* to this world system in which we live. The verb is a present passive imperative exhorting us to cease being caught up in and overwhelmed by the controlled world system. The positive factor in the program is for us to *be continually transformed*. We are to shed ourselves of world conformity; not just to become neutral, but to be changed—to be overhauled in such a way that we take on the characteristics of Christlikeness.

Process (verse 2b). The program of transformation is dependent on the process of mind renewal. Renewed thinking is a process that is basic to renewed living.

Purpose (verse 2c). "That you may prove" is a phrase classified as an infinitive of purpose. The purpose of the mind being renewed is not to amass a lot of wonderful and important facts, but to enable us to "prove what the will of God is." The word "prove" is the Greek term *dokimazo* which has been referred to earlier in this chapter. It carries the idea of testing a substance to determine if it possesses genuine quality. In view here is the activity of the believer with his renewed mind analyzing a given life situation to discern what the will of God is—i.e., to determine the attitude and action proper for that situation. To guard against possible misunderstanding, three adjectives are added to elaborate on the nature of God's will. It is that which is good (as opposed to bad), acceptable (as opposed to displeasing, disappointing), perfect (as opposed to immature, childish).

The renewed mind gives me the *capacity* to be discerning. The world in which I live faces me with the *necessity* of being discerning. I am thinking, feeling, and acting more like Christ—more in harmony with the will of God—and less in conformity with the world system. That's the way the transformation program takes place in my life. It does not happen in some cloistered, isolated retreat center where you have Christian friends, Christian schools, Christian radio, Christian TV, Christian books, Christian magazines, Christian mechanics, Christian stores, Christian yellow pages, etcetera. It happens as you bring your renewed mind and changing life into contact with a world that at best is neutral and more often is hostile. In that environment and under those pressures you grapple with the arduous task of discerning God's will, i.e., what's right and what's wrong. Now, let's see how this works out in some personal, practical situations.

THE FUNCTION OF DISCERNMENT

Let's imagine it is late in the evening. You have had a busy day and are anxious to get home as quickly as you can. You are on a freeway where the traffic is light. The weather is good. The pavement is dry. Your tires and brakes are in fine shape. And there are no patrol cars in sight! You are strongly tempted to drive far in excess of the legal speed limit. But your mind has been renewed with the truth of Romans 13:1— "Let every person be in subjection to the governing authorities." And those authorities put that 55 mph sign there! What you have to do is bring your mind programmed with Romans 13:1 in contact with all of the situational data mentioned above and *discern* what is the right thing to do. You *know* the truth of Romans 13:1. The critical question is—Are you going to *do* the truth of Romans 13:1? To obey Romans 13:1 even when it would be easy and even safe not to will require some healthy discernment. It's up to you.

Or perhaps you are a student with lots of reading, researching and writing to do for a particular course this semester. You also have a part-time job, some responsibilities at church, a couple of other courses you are taking, your own health and well-being to consider, and the need to spend some time with your family. Your mind is deeply conscious of and committed to the concept of walking wisely and redeeming the time (Eph. 5:15-17). What you must do is carefully discern the kind of time schedule which will allow you to get everything done, on time. That won't be easy; it will require ongoing discernment, such as discerning what adjustments to make when your car breaks down, when you are in bed a couple of days with the flu, or when the book you needed was checked out of the library. Without conscious, consistent discernment you will be tempted to do what is fun, or convenient, or easy. With a maturing discernment you will be motivated and enabled to do *what* needs to be done, *when* it needs to be done, and *how* it needs to be done.

Though we are not mechanical robots, we are to function somewhat like a computer. We are to consistently program ourselves with the Word of God. At the same time, our life situations are giving us all kinds of data. We receive it and process it. If we have been or are being programmed by the Word in these areas, we will process it on that basis and our personalized printout will be an indication of what God wants us to be and do in each given situation. Receiving, processing, and deciding are the basic components of discerning.

KNOWING AND GROWING

There you have it—a brief treatise designed to underscore the biblical and practical significance of *discernment*. Teenagers need it. So do adults. Students need it. Faculty likewise. Husbands and wives will find it absolutely essential for marriage. Parents will use it constantly while rearing their kids. We need it to read the paper, to watch television, to talk to friends, to go shopping—in short, to live.

When we use discernment over and over in similar situations, we develop habit patterns, and discernment takes place almost automatically. That's the biblical concept of walking worthy. But God knows we would get complacent if life were totally routine. So He allows new situations to come our way on a fairly regular basis. They keep our discernment skills fresh and growing.

Where we lack discernment, it may be because we aren't regularly assimilating the Word of God into our minds; consequently, we awkwardly fumble around hoping to make the right decision, but lack the perceptive insight we need. Our spiritual clumsiness may be because we've not had a strong, insatiable appetite for the Word of God, which may in turn be caused by eating too much "junk food"—which the world makes readily available, reasonably priced, and so attractively packaged. Or perhaps we have just decided to fast for a season, engaging in a kind of spiritual anorexia, an eating disorder that can stunt our growth and stifle our discernment.

The solution is simple, though not necessarily easy. Like newborn babes we must have an ongoing desire for the Word of God—an appetite that is never completely satisfied. At the same time, we must be functioning as mature adults, increasingly able, in every life-situation, to discern between the good and the bad.

Hebrews 4:12 reminds us that the Word of God is living and active. That is, we are told something about both the nature of the Word of God—it is alive—and the purpose of the Word of God—it is operative. And as a result of what the Word does in us, we are to be operative. The Bible directs our lives, being written in the imperative mood as it were, energizing us and leading us to action. It is the Word of God that lifts our eyes up and out, away from ourselves to our neighbors.

In his meaty little book, The Weight of Glory, *C.S. Lewis draws our attention to this: "The load or weight or burden of my neighbor's glory should be laid daily on my back, a load so heavy that only humility can carry it and the back of the proud will be broken. It's a serious thing to live in a society of possible gods and goddesses, to remember that the dullest and most uninteresting person you talk to may one day be a creature, which, if you saw it now, you would be strongly tempted to worship or else a horror and corruption such as you now meet, if at all, in a nightmare. There are no ordinary people. You have never talked to a mere mortal. Nations, cultures, arts and civilizations—these are mortal and their life is to ours as a life of a gnat, but it is immortals with whom we joke, that we marry, snub, and exploit. Immortal horrors or everlasting splendors. And," says Lewis, "next to the blessed sacrament itself your neighbor is the holiest object presented to your senses."*

Dr. Donald K. Smith, *professor of World Mission at Western Seminary, indicates that after giving us life and strength, the Word of God is to lift our eyes up and out to those around us.*

C H A P T E R   7

THE WORD AS COMMISSION:
Its Missionary Imperative

DONALD K. SMITH

OVER the last seven years I have been particularly concerned for the more than one million people on the east bank of the Nile River in southern Sudan. Ninety years of gospel penetration throughout Africa have failed to reach these thirteen tribes. At first there were no missionaries to go. Then when some went, they were almost totally ignored. At the beginning of seventeen years of civil war they were expelled and almost everything visible of their work was destroyed. The only manuscript of the New Testament for 150,000 people was lost, and the translators were not allowed to reenter. When some missionaries did enter again, an unusual disease forced one family out. Another family was expelled because they had witnessed to and won a Muslim wife to Christ. Bandits ambushed missionary vehicles; one man was shot, but survived. A missionary wife was killed. Fraud in the tiny church crippled its ministry. A Bible school was forced to close because of ambitious grasping for power among its leaders. On and on . . . an incredible chain of defeat.

A Western Seminary graduate of 1984 gained an opportunity to live and work among one of the lost peoples of the East Bank. Then instability reduced the development work of which he was a part. His family was not allowed to join him, and he was captured by rebels. Marvelously his life was spared and he was set free, but spreading chaos forced him out of the land. He and the few others seeking to penetrate that area with the Word of God cannot now return. Airstrips are closed, relief planes have been shot down, and truck convoys with food supplies have been destroyed. After six years of successful famine-stopping development work, two million people of the region face starvation because of the chaotic anarchy.

What senseless rulers who so callously doom people! For what reason? Simply so they can gain and keep power? When did chaos and anarchy begin, and why does it possess wide areas of the world?

THE ORIGIN OF OUR PRESENT CHAOS

Even this present gloom is nothing compared to the blackness that enshrouded the whole world before the entrance of God's Word. When God first shows us the world, the originator of all rebellion held the world in dark subjection. He who had been called the morning star had not a single gleam of light with which he could break apart the darkness. There was no light, no order. His impotence echoed in an empty world. He was prince of this disordered world, and like Tolkien's Gollum he would do anything—everything—to grasp and hold this "Precious." This was his world to be held in doomed subjection, kept away from the glory Elohim intended for it.

Into the center of this rebellion God placed man. Made in God's image and likeness, man shared in God's creative joy, glorifying Him in subduing the earth—restoring order, naming the animals, tending the earth.

Then the enemy subverted God's design; this intolerable intrusion was twisted away from God, and the prince of this world retained his world. Even this creature that had taken dominion from him was subject to him. The light faltered. The initiative was in the hands of darkness. Man had become man's enemy, alienated from the Creator. Satan controlled a re-created world and God's own created man.

· His beauty and power were still revealed in all that He had made—in ordered seasons of sun and rain and growth and harvest, and in the magnificence of a living world. Knowledge of God was present, but that did not break man free from the hateful bondage of rebellion against that God. Nevertheless, God would restore His glorious light to the whole world, and He would do it through man.

Through Noah, God continued His plan to redeem mankind and the whole earth. He renewed man's task in the world, but it was now a limited commission—to multiply, to be fruitful and increase on the earth. Dominion was omitted. Instead, the fear and dread of man replaced the beneficent ordering and tending tasks that God originally gave to man.

GOD'S LIGHT FOR WORLD CHAOS

Then from the wreckage of man, a tiny task force was called out by God to be different from other men. They were a display so the world could begin to learn of God, where the knowledge of what He is like could refute the lies of Satan. Never was the gift of knowledge for these few alone. God's own words made that clear in calling Abraham: "All peoples on earth will be blessed through you" (Genesis 12:3).

Patiently, in century-sized steps, God revealed Himself. The children of Abraham were the cast and the land of Israel the stage where His nature could be seen, where His guiding Word for deliverance from Satan's dark oppression could be demonstrated. "I will also make you a light for the Gentiles, that you may bring my salvation to the ends of the earth" (Isaiah 49:6). Never were the benefits of this drama for the actors and actresses alone. It was an acting out to show the world—divine words lived out to ensure comprehension. But comprehension did not prevent rejection, and the glory that was Israel paled and sank into the gloom of satanic deception and subversion.

How could God speak? The chosen human voices had been stilled; the people had been scattered in their rebellion against God's commands. Golden Jerusalem was littered with rubble and conquerors. God was not in His temple.

Then . . . the Word became flesh. And quietly as light, that Word began to change everything. The darkness could not extinguish the Light, the Son who is the radiance of God's glory.

The Son, God's Word of Light and Glory, shone out with tantalizing splendor in the world of gloom and fear. And He did more than show God's glory; He rescued us from the dominion of darkness. No claim is left against us; we are free to choose the light (John 1:1-18; Hebrews 1:1-5; Colossians 1:10-23).

And that is The Story. God has done the impossible for us. Praise God, we have the Light!

TRANSMITTING THE LIGHT OF THE WORD

Sudan, India, Arabia, Iran, Iraq . . . many places and peoples make up our world. It would be so nice if they were like us, knowing God's Word and enjoying the freedom it brings, wouldn't it?

We were sitting on a shaded porch in southern Sudan, discussing the Bible with a small group of university-trained Sudanese. "What would you do," I asked this elite group, educated to be the leaders of their nation, "if you found an enemy tribesman lying injured beside the path?"

Without hesitation, a science teacher replied, "I'd kill him!" He was somewhat surprised at his own vehemence, so he added, "I'd have to kill him, or my people would kill me as a traitor."

We read the Bible together, about loving your enemies, blessing those who persecute you, giving a cup of cold water, and the Good Samaritan. Soberly, the group confessed, "That's what the Bible says all right. It's very, very difficult to follow the Bible—but that's the only thing that would make a difference in our land."

These men had been bound—by their clan, their tribe, their race—to kill. They had not heard the Word that God speaks.

> Where cross the crowded ways of life,
> Where sound the cries of race and clan,
> Above the noise of selfish strife
> We hear Thy voice, O Son of Man.

No, The Story does not stop with salvation's light for us. That is only the midpoint in The Story of which all other stories are only tiny parts.

The Word was the Son of man, the Second Adam, a new beginning of a new race. Freedom from sin, yes, and stunning liberation from the confines of family, clan, nation and man's racialism. "Here there is no Greek or Jew, circumcised or uncircumcised, barbarian, Scythian, slave or free, but Christ is all, and is in all" (Colossians 3:11). We are no longer bound to kill our enemies; the Living Word gives us the liberty to love all men.

We are part of a new race, through which the fulfillment of the Plan of the Ages will be worked. The authority and dominion granted to man in the first great commission and lost by Adam is restored in the Second Adam. That authority is specifically shared by Jesus Christ in the recommissioning of God's children, the new race: "All authority in heaven and on earth has been given to me. Therefore go . . . . And surely I will be with you always. . . ."

It is the Word that simultaneously restores authority and impels His children into every part of the world, to every man.

THE UNIVERSAL NEED OF THE WORD

There are many reasonable objections to this. What right do we have to interfere with someone else's religion? How dare we alter another's culture? Aren't you just moved by pity and a certain satisfied superiority? We don't know what's best for someone else. We can't even handle the problems in our own society.

Georgie Ann Geyer emphasizes our national moral impotence. She traces the decay and fall of great cultures, a decay associated with wide use of drugs—in Persia, among the Incas, in the forgotten beauty of Yemen, and in the China on which opium was forced. Then she concludes:

> Is it not frighteningly odd that this most blessed of countries [the United States] should not have drugs forced upon it like the Chinese, but should accept them by choice? Is it not fearsome that so many in this country . . . should actually choose oblivion?

> The questions I am hearing are: "How do we deal with this?" and "How do we educate Americans against drugs?" The question I would like to see addressed is, "Why? Why, in God's name, is it happening on this scale, in this country, in this time, with a people who have so much and so many choices?"

The answer is simple: We have not allowed ourselves to grow as new men, a new race. Our knowledge, even about holy things, is often shadowed and we have little sense of the Absolute.

In confusion shown by the enemy, it is only the Word that gives knowledge of the Absolute. It is the Word that shows us God's purpose, that gives understanding of the cosmic conflict and our role in it. It is the Word that draws us outward, away from ourselves, so we can introduce all men to God's new family and race through the wonder of the new birth.

Without the Word, we would know none of this. We would be protectively isolated in our separate clans and races, mis-

takenly revering tradition alone, because we knew nothing
more. We would have no criteria for truth. We would be suffo-
cated with disinformation. We would have no authority to act
against the effects of sin, and against the powers of sin and
darkness. We would have no hope, no message.

We would have no care for God's whole world. It is God's
Word alone that pulls us outward to others, at the same time
giving us the fixed reference point that provides our only certainty as we travel in unknown patterns of living. It is the
universality of that Word that gives understanding as we go in
unmeasured and unbuilt ways, among people whom we do not
know and where we do not understand the guidelines.

God's Word, not sympathy for the diseased and hungry,
pulls us out. Those who are alone, empty of God and hope,
trapped in a thousand-and-one resentments, bitternesses and
angers, are everywhere. Without the Word, sputtering emotions
would never stir us to reach those groping in darkness. Emotion
is never enough to carry us through the hardship, loneliness
and rejection that may well be our experience when we oppose
the dark powers of this world.

No, the Living Word in us gives us not only a Message,
but the authority and courage to fully and faithfully proclaim
that Message. When God chose to speak to man, He did not
preach a sermon, send a tract or develop a media program. He
gave a life. The Word became flesh, deeply involved with men,
sharing their language, experience, culture, and seeing to the
very core of their values and false assumptions.

It is the Word become flesh that heals the sick, feeds the
hungry, fills empty and lonely places, that today can bring
order out of chaos. It is this Word that gives an understandable
human voice to God's call, "Come unto Me all you that labor
and are heavy-laden, and I will give you rest."

O Master, from the mountain side
Make haste to heal these hearts of pain;
Among these restless throngs abide,
O tread the city streets again.

Till sons of men shall learn Thy love
And follow where Thy feet have trod—
Till glorious, from Thy heav'n above
Shall come the city of our God.

Is our mission to the world the *end*, then, of God's purposes for us? By no means! We have been formed for a glorious
role in God's eternal kingdom. Salvation is not the final end
of God's design for men; nor is missions that final calling of
men. These are steps to glory, the glory we will share forever
with the Divine Word:

> With your blood you purchased men for God from every
> tribe and language and people and nation. You have made
> them to be a kingdom and priests to serve our God, and
> they will reign on the earth. (Revelation 5:9-10)

This is the denouement of the divine drama encompassing
the world: The new race, the new creation in Christ, will rule
in this world in the place of those who rebelled and who angrily
skulk in the shadowed gloom of the enemy. But those dark
powers will concede defeat and even in their doom acknowledge with all creation that Jesus, the Word, is Lord:

> I heard every creature in heaven and on earth and under
> the earth and on the sea, and all that is in them, singing:
> To him who sits on the throne and to the Lamb be praise
> and honor and glory and power, forever and ever!
> (Revelation 5:13)

Scientists alarm us. They tell us that we are living in the very heart of a colossal, cosmic explosion in which all of the stuff of the universe is rushing headlong into the outer recesses of space, out of control. Most of us would not deny that at times our own personal lives seem to confirm that sense of being unconnected, out of control.

Certainly, down in the inner recesses of all men there is a deep longing for that "something" that can provide cohesion and meaning for life. What is rooted in men of all nations and cultures is a desperate sense of needing to belong, a need to feel at one with others and with God. The great counterpart to man's sense of disconnectedness lies in the grace of God who draws us to a sense of belonging. God has provided for man's need, and the Bible speaks to that inner longing.

Believers rejoice in belonging to the Body of Christ, and in the unity which is to characterize that Body. Yet we recognize the many theological and practical problems with which the church has been faced as it has declared that truth. Is there in reality any hope of unity?

In this chapter, Professor **James W. Andrews,** *chairman of the Division of Ministerial Studies and assistant professor of Homiletics at Western Seminary, describes for us the Bible's role in unifying believers. By its truth and on its terms we can experience belonging and unity in Christ.*

THE WORD AS UNIFIER:
Its Unifying Power

JAMES W. ANDREWS

Y EARS ago as a young pastor I had opportunity at a conference to converse a few minutes privately with Dr. Carl F. H. Henry. We were talking about theological perspective and how hard it is to stay in the biblical mainstream in the midst of doctrinal controversy. He gave me some wise counsel which I will always remember (though I fear I have often neglected). His words were approximately these:

"In my opinion," he said, "we ought to take our cue from the apostolic drummers. Let us find the great themes they rivet on and let us hammer on those. That, it seems to me, is the best way to stay in the biblical mainstream and avoid the deadend streets of theological tangents and personal hobby horses."

MAJORING ON MINORS

We Christians have a notorious habit of majoring on minors. Let me illustrate.

In at least fifteen chapters of Pauline literature alone, concern for spiritual unity dominates the atmosphere. In addition, I have noted at least ten other chapters where directives regarding unity are in one form or another present or prominent.

We tend to give far more treatment to other issues about which the Bible says far less. Think for a second about some of the subjects we get all steamed about these days. Today you can always find an ear ready for such topics as abortion, capital punishment, church worship, church polity, church discipline, qualifications for elders, marriage, divorce, child-rearing and the like.

All these themes and others are both legitimate and relevant matters for Christian concern. Yet, I would point out, none of them receives the New Testament attention that this issue of unity does.

A Surprising Fact

To take the contrast one step further, it may surprise you to learn that epistolary literature in the New Testament places significantly less emphasis on the duty of personal evangelism outside the Church than upon the obligation of personal alignment in the Church.

That observation in no way is intended to minimize the importance of personal evangelism in our Christian agenda. I desire merely by contrast to underscore the strategic importance the New Testament places on the maintenance of Christian unity within the Body.

In slighting this emphasis, we could be straining at gnats and swallowing camels. If Satan can divert believers from biblical majors to biblical minors, he has won a tactical victory. That cannot do the Church any good. The judgments of God are sometimes subtle. The chickens always come home to roost in one way or another.

ACCOUNTING FOR THE APATHY

How do we account for our chronic apathy about this issue? The answer is important, for it locates the roots of resistance in ourselves and where we need to start in rectifying our condition.

First, let us consider the roots of our apathy. What accounts for our indifference and chronic irresponsibility in promoting and practicing this ideal?

No small part of the problem is our modern *climate of individualism*. We live in a culture that exalts individualism to what British scholar J. A. Walter calls a "sacred." A sacred is a functional (as opposed to formal) idol. It is an ultimate value to which people are committed, and one which imparts to people their sense of meaning. Walter writes:

> In an individualistic society, a person gains a sense of identity through uniqueness and individuality. This entails emphasizing the differences between myself and others, distinguishing myself from others . . . . The conformist is looked down upon, and the person who distinguishes himself from others is admired . . . .

> But distinguishing oneself in more socially acceptable ways also entails costs for others. To distinguish oneself by becoming top dog means that someone else has to be bottom dog; if I am superior then someone else has to be inferior. (*Sacred Cows,* pp. 94-95.)

That hallmark of contemporary society is one of the most centrifugal influences in group life. Individualism is a habit of mind that has to be different, at least, and wants to appear to be superior, if possible. The demand to be different sets us apart from one another and the desire to be superior sets us at odds with one another.

Is there no place in Christian unity for individuality then? Let us not confuse indivdualism with individuality.

What is the difference? Individualism is difference by design. It is a difference selfishly motivated and self-consciously flaunted. Individuality is difference by nature, spontaneous and unpretentious. Individuality is diversity compatible with unity. Individualism is deviation incompatible with harmony.

Other factors (such as our obsession with individual rights versus individual responsibility, our modern distrust of authority and memories of self-serving leaders who suppress legitimate dissent on pious pretexts) also contribute to some of our neglect of this important theme.

A DEFINITION PROBLEM

Aside from our apathy toward the topic, one of the major difficulties we have in discussing it is *definitional*. The term "unity" carries too much baggage. It means too many different things to different people. That leads to false starts and false standards and unrealistic expectations.

So our primary intention in this message is to answer this question: *What is meant by Christian unity?* What are its essential components? How do we know when we have a spirit of Christian unity or lack it? And in greater or lesser measure? Only when we understand the issue at the conceptual level can we make progress toward that dispositional spirit of oneness that the New Testament constantly appeals for.

Before I spell out what I believe Christian unity is, let me first tell you what it isn't. For the sake of clarity we need to dispose of some common but false notions in circulation today.

MISCONCEPTION: ORGANIZATIONAL UNIFICATION

First of all, do not confuse the Christian unity with *organization unification*. The ecumenical movement makes this equation constantly, appealing to John 17 where Jesus in His high priestly prayer prayed to His Father that

> they may all be one even as Thou, Father, art in Me, and
> I in Thee, that they also may be in Us, that the world
> may believe that Thou didst send Me. And the glory
> which Thou hast given Me I have given to them; that
> they may be one just as We are one, I in them, and Thou
> in Me, that they may be perfected in unity, that the world
> may know that Thou didst send Me, and didst love them,
> even as Thou didst love Me. (17:21-22)

Incidentally, isn't it a curious inconsistency that men who otherwise reject the Scripture as their authoritative rule of faith and practice, in this instance appeal to the Word for their mandate to amalgamate? One cannot help suspect the piety of their motives when their appeals to biblical authority are so selective.

But motives aside, what about the validity of their interpretation of Jesus' prayer for oneness?

That prayer, I believe, has no reference to formal organizational unity or homogeneity. I believe a close reading of the text requires us to understand Jesus' petition as referring to either (1) a oneness already accomplished through the cross and the agency of the Holy Spirit, or (2) an ideal, eschatological (final or end-time) oneness yet to be realized when Christ returns—or, most likely, both of the above. Why?

(1) Because Jesus' prayers are failsafe. His prayers never fail to be answered. He always prays according to the will of God. His petitions and His Father's designs are always in perfect lockstep. It is inconceivable that He offered to the Father such a magnificent petition as a mere wish. Did He Himself not attest to His Father in the raising of Lazarus, "I knew that Thou hearest Me always"? No, here Jesus transcends an unfulfilled wish. His petition has not gone begging because of the obstreperousness of the fallen men He bought with His blood and is still renewing in His likeness.

(2) What Jesus requested is couched in *organic* rather than in *institutional* terms. "That they may be one even as Thou, Father, art in Me, and I in Thee, that they may be also

in Us." Now, is the oneness of the Father and Son of an organic or organizational nature? Is it internal or external? Is it formal or essential? Obviously, the organizational analogy doesn't fit the language of the prayer.

(3) The achievement of a monolithic organization would not achieve the object of His petition. Note the purpose of this oneness: "that the world may know that Thou didst send Me, and didst love them, even as Thou didst love Me" (verse 23). How would the reunification of all churches prove to the world that the mission of Christ was indeed from God and that the Church is the object of Divine love? The only thing that will prove those things is the appearance of the Bridegroom from heaven and the glorious revelation of His bride, the Church. Then the world will know! Until then they will not get the message no matter how formally unified the Church may be.

(4) Notice that the oneness Jesus envisions requires for its realization the impartation of the glory with which the Father has invested Him.

> And the glory which Thou hast given Me I have given
> to them; that they may be one just as We are one, I in
> them, and Thou in Me, that they may be perfected in
> unity. (17:22-23)

This, I believe, refers to the bestowment of the Holy Spirit. The God-man, Jesus, was endued with the Spirit without measure. In His earthly ministry we see him impelled into the wilderness by the Spirit.

Others (possibly correctly) construe the reference to His glory differently. Godet, for example, sees it as an allusion to His adoption. Meyer takes it more broadly of investing believers with His heavenly glory, the first fruits of which is realized now in the Spirit, and His benefits and the rest held in trust until the second advent. This view is consistent with the narrower reference I have taken, but it is hard to be dogmatic.

Whatever view one takes, the gift of the Spirit is a necessary entailment. Endowment of the Holy Spirit is a prerequisite for the oneness Jesus requests. But the liberal interpretation sees Him asking for a unity that requires only negotiation, not inward transformation.

To the extent His petition has been fulfilled, the oneness has two manifestations.

Shared Privileges. One aspect is a unity expressed in the *shared privileges of royal pedigree.* This bond of privilege is not the essence of what Christ prayed for, but its effulgence. It is a magnificent mutuality of relationship that exists because of God's grace. Its existence depends in no way on our feelings or recognition or affiliations.

Our unity in this form is *positional, not dispositional.* These privileges are a bond that unites believers of every race, gender, age, class, and denomination.

And what is this opulent cosmic commonalty that unites believers? In Ephesians 4:3-6 it is described as "the unity of the Spirit," consisting in these shared benefits:

> There is one body and one Spirit—just as you were called
> to one hope when you were called—one Lord, one faith,
> one baptism; one God and Father of all, who is over all
> and through all and in all.

As a result, the Church enjoys a certified oneness that may be obscured by disharmony, but one that can never be obliterated by dissension.

Organic Interdependency. The other aspect of this objective unity consists in a *complex interdependency within a shared life source.*

What Jesus had in mind, then, was not the sort of institutional or organizational amalgamation that the Consultation on Church Union envisions. While His petition does not necessarily preclude that as an expression of this oneness, it certainly does not require it either. Rather, the burden of His petition was a *spiritual* rather than a *formal* integration. Jesus' concern was for *functional* oneness rather than *structural* homogeneity.

In Christ dead men in Adam are animated with the Spirit

of God through whom they are joined as living organisms to the spiritual Body of Christ. Therein we participate in the divine nature and enjoy divine privileges. We enjoy through the Holy Spirit a living connection with Christ, such as a living branch has with a vital vine. The oneness He sought has been realized in part in the glorious symmetry and organized interdependence of the Body of Christ described in Ephesians 4:16.

> From him [Christ] the whole body, joined and held
> together by every supporting ligament, grows and builds
> itself up in love, as each part does its work.

MISCONCEPTION: LOCAL CHURCH HARMONY

Second, let us not confuse Christian unity with local church harmony. It is easy to make that equation. But it leads to all kinds of confusion.

But surely, you say, a spirit of Christian unity will engender an atmosphere of Christian harmony.

Ah now, that is a different matter! Did you catch the distinction? There is a vast difference in saying that spiritual unity will produce harmony among believers and saying that it will bring about harmony in the Church. If we begin to measure the appropriateness of beliefs and behaviors by what produces peace in the Church versus what promotes harmony among genuine believers, we will invariably find ourselves cutting the corners of truth and holiness as a shortcut to a cheap peace that we mistake for Christian unity.

We must come to terms with the fact that the modern Church in its visible, organized form is an unholy mixture of wheat and tares. The outward Church is a mixed multitude. There will never be peace and harmony between believers and unbelievers, no matter how imbued with religion they happen to be. There is no inner compatibility. Divisions will always surface between men of God and men of the world. Whatever the New Testament says about being of one mind and having one purpose and one love, it speaks to men of faith who belong to the Body of Christ, not men of the flesh who happen to hold membership in some local manifestation of that Body.

Church harmony merely indicates a state of peaceful relations among the members of a local organization. Christian unity indicates a state of right relations to the Head of the Body and to the members of His Body. There is a vast difference between those two things.

Some Christian leaders may be in for a shock. Praised by men for their ability to keep the peace, one day they may have to give account to God for the kind of peace they have settled for.

There is a peace of God and there is a peace of the flesh. A carnal peace comes at the expense of the truth, but a godly peace by means of it. A carnal peace is preserved by evading Christian duty, but a godly peace by fulfulling it. A carnal peace is won by bowing to the pressures of willful men, but a godly peace is achieved by deferring to a holy God.

Said Bishop J. D. Ryle:

> Unity in the abstract is no doubt an excellent thing: but unity without truth is useless. Peace and uniformity are beautiful and valuable: but peace without the Gospel— peace based on a common Episcopacy, and not a common faith—is a worthless peace, not deserving the name. (*Knots Untied*, p. 319.)

A church can have peace simply because nobody cares. There are more than a few of those whose convictions are so limp that no truth is worth getting bruised over. And there are those who are so persistent in forcing the truth on the conscience of the unwilling that they bring up the mud in the church's character bucket. When that happens some pusillanimous pastor named Ahab who cares only to run the course in comfort and complacency will invariably condemn the Elijah as a "troubler of Israel."

There can be no spiritual communion where there is no spiritual union. There can be no inner conformity of human spirit where there is no mutual relation to the Holy Spirit.

ESSENTIAL ELEMENTS OF DISPOSITIONAL UNITY

Now we know what Christian unity isn't. Let us now define what it *is* in the dispositional sense (as distinct from the positional form). What are its components that mark its presence or absence, vitality or debility?

I have sifted the New Testament carefully for clues. My study has focused on those contexts where we have explicit appeals for Christian unity. I think we can narrow it down to three indispensable elements.

A spirit of Christian unity, I believe, entails:

(1) *A shared commitment to the gospel of Christ.*

In one of Paul's appeals for unity in Philippians 1:27, note how clearly this aspect is present.

> Only let your citizenship be worthy of the gospel of
> Christ, in order that whether I come and see you or remain
> absent, I might hear with respect to the things that concern
> you, that you are standing firm in one spirit, with one
> soul striving together for the faith of the gospel.

Many things, not all of them good, can bring people together around a common cause. The Pharisees and Sadducees united in the crucifixion of Jesus. Pilate and Herod, two antagonists, became friends because Pilate remanded Jesus at His arraignment to the jurisdiction of Herod.

However, to qualify as Christian unity, there must be mutual allegiance to the gospel. And by "gospel" is meant, of course, the gospel according to the apostolic witness, not the liberal tradition.

Where there is true spiritual unity (as opposed to mere external peace or some other basis of unanimity) the proclamation of the gospel dominates the heart's agenda. Like Paul in

Philippians 1:18 we care only that Christ is proclaimed in truth. (see also Romans 16:17.)

(2) *A shared affection for Christ and His own.*

If the first bond of Christian unity is a common faith in the gospel of Christ, the second tie that binds is a common feeling for Christ and those that are joined to Him.

In Philippians 2:2, Paul admonishes the Macedonians to make his joy full "by being of the same mind, maintaining the same love, united in spirit, intent on one purpose." Note the emphasis on maintaining the "same love." What does this mean? Paul's concern here seems related more to the threat of diversity than to weakness of intensity. In context I believe the point is to fixate on the same object of affection.

Christian love is at bottom an affection for Christ irradiated in our being by the Holy Spirit. It extends its feeling for Him to all that is His. But this sentiment is as much a motion as it is an emotion, as much a lifestyle as it is a heartbeat. At its roots it is a way of feeling about Christ. But in its expression it is a way of responding to Him and to His.

It is that behavioral feature of this affection that Paul had in mind in Colossians 3:14. There after exhorting the Church to go beyond mere stoic tolerance of the weak and the offensive, he urges them to "put on love which," he adds, "is the bond of perfection."

Note that love is indeed a bonding influence. It is "perfect" in the sense that, in the words of John Eadie, it unites all graces in the ideal blend and proportion. Love is a galvanizing behavior that draws its energy from holy roots of affection for Christ together with all He loves and claims. Where this affection is mutually shared, its behavior is mutually observed and Christian hearts are "knit together in love." (Colossians 2:2)

(3) *A shared commitment to please God.*

A third essential component of Christian unity is a common purpose. Note how in Philippians 2:2, Paul urges the Philippians to be intent on one purpose. Although not as plain in the English translation as it could be, this telic aspect of Christian unity is present in all those passages, including this one, which appeals for believers to have the same mind—passages such as Romans 15:5-6 and 1 Corinthians 1:10. The Greek words have the connotation of purpose or intention.

The mission of Christ was to glorify His Father. His purpose is supposed to be our priority. Christian unity cannot coexist with private agendas.

SUMMARY

So then, Christian unity or concord exists when there is a mutual consent to an apostolic doctrine (i.e., to the gospel), to apostolic devotion (i.e., affection for Christ and His Church), and to an apostolic design in life (i.e., pleasing God) . . . a common faith, a common feeling, a common function.

Therein lie the essential ingredients of Christian unity. As long as we are bonded at these points we have the equation of unity. For such a unity will admit disagreement, diversity, and even disunion. What it cannot admit is dissension. The spirit of dissension sows discord through hidden agendas and pious deception.

We might distinguish disagreement and dissension this way: Disagreement is merely a dispute among believers with different perceptions in behalf of common commitments. Dissension is a dispute among people with different agendas without regard to mutual duty.

Nothing about Christian unity precludes differences of opinion, taste, or style; what is really ruled out is difference of conviction, affection and intention.

HARD QUESTIONS

Now that we better understand the essence of the spirit we call "Christian unity," we cannot evade its inner logic.

Can people who are so bonded tolerate the kind of structural fragmentation that implies (and in many cases involves) alienation and competition? Is it not hypocritical to postulate the possibility of a "dispositional" unity that balks at organizational unity? Is not the refusal to unite at the formal level prima facie evidence that something is amiss at the feeling level? Can we claim to pursue a spirit of unity and stop short of structural union? These questions press for an honest answer.

Let us distinguish at least two types of division we see on the modern church horizon.

(1) There are breaches that arise from fidelity to a biblical faith. Some fissures are undesirable, but essential. I am talking about those unfortunate situations where churches fall hopelessly under the control of unbelief. To break away from such churches is not a separation from the Church, but a retreat to it. By its apostasy the denomination had ceased to be a church except in name.

Spiritual unity, as we have noted, requires a common conviction, affection, and intention. Where those foundations are lacking, there is no biblical basis for unity. Again, there can be no unity of the human spirit where there is nothing in common with the Holy Spirit. In such cases the scandal is not to separate, but to remain unequally yoked.

A church which has ceased to believe the Word has lost its license. It is no longer accredited by Heaven. It should no longer be acknowledged by its citizens. In such cases it must be understood that the division was in those leaving the faith, not in those leaving the fold.

What Jesus asked for is not something that organizational solidarity can necessarily achieve. In fact, in some cases it may not even rightly express it. For any union of the members that disrupts communion with their Head is not a sign of spiritual health, but of spiritual sickness. Any form of union that weakens the spiritual vitality of the members is not the work of the Paraclete, but rather the effect of a parasite. In the Body of Christ what is most crucial is a sound relationship to the Head. When the Head controls the members, the Body pulls together and each member contributes its appropriate part to the directives of the Head (Colossians 2:19).

(2) There are divisions rooted in godless frictions and self-serving agendas.

Unfortunately this category accounts for far too much of the fragmentation and redundancy of churches and parachurch ministries that have proliferated all over the face of modern evangelicalism. It is indeed a scandal which erodes our credibility.

We welcome communion in many cases, but we are threatened by union. We find too much of our identity in the community rather than in Christ. A loss of institutional identity jeopardizes our personal identity. Hence an unhealthy privatism in which the organization is more than a means to a spiritual end. Although we cover the reality with pious froth, the fact is that our institutional affiliation has become an idol. What we believe in most, what we are most devoted to is the organization, not the organism.

True, in many instances a good case might be made for the status quo. However, we need to recognize that there is no good excuse for it. We salve our conscience with cooperation. But if our hearts were harnessed to the same plow, we should be talking about integration. Maybe it is time for evangelicals to take stock and see if we are all in the same row.

We therefore must condemn the unconscionable facility with which we divide and persist in our rivalries. I have no doubt that a true spirit of Christian unity, such as I earlier defined, would indeed break down many of the organizational, emotional, and peripheral doctrinal walls that divide us. If we cannot justify our separate maintenance on grounds of faith or function, maybe we ought to question the purity of our spiritual allegiance.

I think we might be wise to consider ourselves guilty until proven innocent. Far too many churches and parachurch agencies owe their autonomous existence not to strategic need, but simply to ego, error or eccentricity.

OUR RESPONSIBILITY

What then is our responsibility before the Word of God about this issue of Christian unity?

(1) Let us examine our hearts. Does the spirit of Christian unity really inhabit us? Can we honestly profess that we believe the gospel with all our hearts, that Christ and His Church are the objects of our paramount devotion and that pleasing God is our chief ambition in life? Until we can look into the face of God and affirm those sentiments with a clear conscience, we are part of the problem, not part of the solution. The seeds of discord lurk in our hearts.

(2) Let us quit conning ourselves concerning our commitment. More often than we admit, it is not our commitment to the apostolic faith that splinters us. It is not our lack of passion for Christ and His Church or a singleminded intention to accomplish His work that keeps us wastefully duplicating expensive buildings and other resources. Too often it is our hidden agendas that keep us walled up and make us competitors rather than co-laborers.

(3) Let us show the propriety of our divisions rather than merely continue to rationalize them. In this respect, we are guilty until proven innocent. If we don't need to separate or remain divided for some compelling reason compatible with our commitments, let us close ranks and heal the breaches. Diversity has its place and may even complement unity. It is sometimes necessary to maintain the faith. But how many of our divisions can honestly be justified as essential to our basic commitments to the faith?

The bottom line is that we evangelicals have often given the Lord's appeal for unity rather short shrift. We need to be reminded that the judgments of God are not partial. They sometimes prove to be subtle time bombs. The wise will take heed and be warned by the Word. It challenges those who would be productive for Christ to doggedly pursue the kind of unity for which He prayed in His final appeal to the Father. Before such unity no foe can stand.

Several years ago America watched a television program which was to make a broad and significant impact on the nation. The program, "Roots," quite unexpectedly set in motion among us some deep and hidden impulse to uncover our connections with our personal histories. Suddenly we were rushing to the corner genealogist, looking for the story that explained who we are and how we got here. Perhaps it was a case of personal history having to suffice because of our inability to come to grips with the whole of history. Most moderns wrestle with the fact of history, sensing perhaps that attempts at understanding history mean facing ultimate reality.

The problem of history has turned many of the brightest men and women into cynics. Napoleon once said that history is merely a set of lies agreed upon. Historian Ariel Durant offered the observation that "history is mostly guessing, and rest is bias." Carl Sandburg put it succinctly: "History is a bucket of ashes." And Henry Ford was at least as terse: "History is bunk."

Only Christians can ultimately escape the perplexing problem of history, because they see the God of the past as the God of eternity. Anglican theologian John Stott said that as Christians we still face a painful tension with regard to history. "Some Christians, anxious above all else to be faithful to the revelation of God without compromise, ignore the challenges of the modern world around them, trim and twist God's revelation in their search for relevance. Christians are at liberty to surrender neither to antiquity nor to modernity; we are to submit to the revelation of yesterday within the realities of today."

Dr. H. Crosby Englizian, professor of Historical Theology at Western Seminary, teaches us the importance of the Word of God in its historical dimension, giving us a platform from which to look toward eternity.

THE WORD AS HISTORY:
Its Historical Base

H. CROSBY ENGLIZIAN

THE bishop of Durham, England, raised a stir in 1984 among his fellow Anglicans by voicing doubts that Jesus' virgin birth and resurrection are historical facts. The House of Bishops responded by affirming that "Christianity is a house built on the rock of actual events" (*Christianity Today,* July 11, 1986).

Those actual events we believe to be recorded in the Bible, a gracious and redemptive revelation from God to man. We affirm, therefore, that revelation is something which has happened!

We would agree with Professor Machen that though some of the *ideas* of Scripture may be found elsewhere in other faiths, these ideas would not make them Christian faiths nor would the experiences of their followers be Christian for the simple reason that Christian faith and experience rest upon biblical historical happenings (Machen, *Christianity and Liberalism,* 71).

BIBLE HISTORY A REVELATION OF GOD

That God has revealed Himself in history is well secured in the history of the Old Testament Hebrews. Israel's existence and self-understanding were rooted in the belief that God's purposes for them were being worked out in historical events. This could not be true of other ancient peoples. The Greeks, for example, found little of enduring significance in their history. Ancient historiographers could not do what the Scriptures have done: to declare a unity, design, and meaning within history.

God by nature is necessarily active in the world: speaking, communicating, redeeming, judging. This is an affirmation fundamental to the whole of Scripture. Historian Herbert Butterfield has stated, "Christianity is historical religion because it presents us with religious doctrines which are at the same time historical events or historical interpretations" (Ronald H. Nash, *Christian Faith and Historical Understanding*, 11).

Perhaps most remarkably, God is revealed as active even in lives and events which would outwardly deny Him. Slavery and exile, the evils of wicked emperors, the ravaging conquests of ancient rulers—all are declared to be God's instruments. Nebuchadnezzar is His servant; Cyrus, His chosen one (Jeremiah 25:9, Isaiah 44:28). Our all-powerful Sovereign has determined to glorify Himself through historical thick and historical thin.

As much as it is man's nature to hide, it is God's nature to unveil and to seek. He is the primary actor in the drama of biblical history. Though His glory is set above the created order, He is integrally involved in it—with real people and their fearsome struggles, with marauding tribes, with lovers, with orphans and widows. Though God's revelation has come in diverse ways over many centuries, through Old Testament prophets and finally in His Son, all of it is within the context of human history. One cannot look upon the brightly painted and garish, mute gods of the nations without thinking thankfully: "My God speaks. He speaks to me. And in speaking, He acts."

"He spoke and it was done; He commanded and it stood fast" (Psalm 33:9). Bernard Ramm has written, "The word is the hard datum in the area of truth; the event is the hard datum in the area of history" (ETS, v. 14, pt. 2, Spring 1971, Amaya, p. 73). The historical event and the truthful word are to be equally and necessarily affirmed. This is the message of our text in Hebrews 1:1-2 which provides our theme: The Word as History (see Hebrews 4:12). We address it from three viewpoints: the historical, hermeneutical, and theological.

HISTORY INDISPENSABLE TO REVELATION

Let's first note the historical, especially in the face of the centuries-long devaluation of history. History has always had a poor reputation. "History is a great dust heap." "History is a myth that men agree to believe." Someone else, who understandably remains anonymous, said, "Happy is the country that has not history."

Our text presents God as an eternal Person who chose to enter into a time/space relationship with physical things and with sinful persons. Whether by creative, providential, incarnational, or judicial acts, He has initiated certain actions. Neither an abstraction nor an idol, He is a person; and, as all other persons, He unveils Himself by His words and deeds. We are not saying the Bible is God's history: for one thing, He has done far more than is recorded. But the Bible is God's self-disclosure, designed to disclose itself in historical terms.

We must insist therefore that the historical events recorded in Old and New Testaments are indispensable to revelation. Other world religions also might claim historicity, but Christianity maintains that its God has revealed His truth through specific individuals, not the least of which is Christ, and through many events, all of which bear the meaning and value which He has given to them.

When God spoke by the prophets and in His Son, He made history. When the Word became flesh, He made history. Bernard Ramm has stated, "Revelation comes by the history-making power of the Word of God" (*Special Revelation on the Word of God,* 70). A real crucifixion is a necessary condition to its truth value. Christian faith in the resurrection of Jesus requires an empty gravesite.

Should our confidence in this history be compromised, revelation would be weakened. In the preface to his Gospel, Saint Luke sets out in chapter one to write a historical narrative of "things most surely believed among us." He immediately writes of King Herod, priest Zacharias, wife Elizabeth, and several other family related matters. Chapter two continues with Caesar Augustus. This is factual history necessary to faith; it is not some kind of meta-history.

A professional historian has stated, "There are four essential ingredients in the study of history and without them there would be no written history" (Alan W. Brownsward; "Doing History: A Skills Approach," *The History Teacher,* Vol. 6, No. 2, Feb. 1973, 252). These are evidence, definitions, interpretation, and values. "Without evidence there would be no written history, and without definition of terms there would be no written history worth understanding, for interpretation means trying to give meaning to evidence" (p. 257).

God is the master historiographer to include these four elements in the sacred record and thereby lend historical credibility to the record and to underscore the profound significance of this particular historical past. Luke said he was writing "an orderly account . . . that you may know the certainty of those things in which you were instructed" (Luke 1:3-4). An orderly account would necessarily incorporate these same ingredients.

A chief value of written history then is its documentation of factual happenings—of evidence. Myths and fables may be occasional avenues of morals, but they cannot do what the historical record alone can do. Robert Rendall says, "Faith in Christ is more than the acceptance of His teachings: It is the acceptance of Him *as He is presented to us in the Scriptures* of both Testaments. Faith is rooted in historical fact" (*History, Prophecy, and God*, p. 20; emphasis mine).

This was surely true of Israel's faith, which rested on God's fidelity to the Abrahamic covenant, on the exodus from Egypt, and the eventual incarnation of Messiah, necessary consequences of that historic covenant. (By that ancient covenant, New Testament history is linked with Old Testament history, and Jesus Christ with the ancient fathers, making for magnificent unity, continuity, progress, and goal—all necessary elements in any authoritative historiography.) "I am the first and the last; and beside Me there is no God" (Isaiah 44:6). "I am God and there is none like Me; declaring the end from the beginning, and from ancient times the things that are not yet done" (Isaiah 46:9-10). The creative-redemptive God is the quintessential historiographer. As such, He must communicate Himself historically.

HISTORY INDISPENSABLE TO INTERPRETATION

The Bible's history is also important as a hermeneutical guide. In addition to factual evidence, good written history requires interpretation through definition and explanation. Without an internally coherent interpretation, biblical events would hardly be worth reading. "A bare historical incident is not a divine revelation. . . . For the acts of God to be revelatory, not only the acts but the meaning of events also must be divinely disclosed" (*What the Bible Teaches about the Bible*, H. D. McDonald, 26). Leon Morris echoes: "Deeds by themselves are not revelation" (quoted by McDonald). History to be revelatory requires explanation; God in His wisdom and purpose has provided this. We are not left to wild imaginings, to do with the facts what we choose, as with the modern cults. Mormons read the Bible and teach that Christ is essentially no different that we; hence, His incarnation is not unique nor does His atonement provide salvation for all. To Mrs. Eddy, Jesus was only a man, and Christ is an idea. With such an under-standing, who needs Him? And of what value is the Arian, created Christ of the Jehovah's Witnesses (*Four Major Cults*, A. Hoekema, 382)? The God of Scripture not only acts, He communicates cosmic significance.

He spoke clearly to Israel in such ways that they under-stood exactly why events were transpiring as they were (see Deuteronomy 9:4-6 and 4:32-40). The Scriptures tell us Jesus died on a cross; they then tell us why—"for our sins" (Romans 4:25). The Milanese Bishop Ambrose refers to the inspired Word of revelation as history and mystery: i.e., events and meaning of events. That God *explains* the history tells us that the interpretation is neither broad nor inconsequential, and indeed is one in which He is intimately and redemptively re-lated.

He who was operative in Old Testament history—the Eternal—became flesh.

In the "paroxysm of divine effort" (James Conolly, *Human History and the Word of God*, 228), Christ was shown to be the decisive life in biblical history. As Rendall states it, "The interpretive point of Old Testament history is Christ" (Luke 24:44, Hebrews 9:26). Indeed, of all history. B.C. and A.D. are more than chronological symbols; to us they represent re-velatory interpretation (Ephesians 1:10).

We may look at this matter of interpreting history from the standpoint of memory, and agree to two axioms: (1) the human race cannot live without memory; (2) history is essential to memory.

Now, our memories are not required to provide plenary recall, despite some history teachers, but only those more sig-nificant events as determined by our interpretations. As the general historian provides interpretation along with his narra-tive, so God in the Bible has done the same. By this He would teach us what is significant in human affairs, and, with our Christian lives in view, that it is an interpreted history which alone produces behavioral change. God's people have been constantly reminded to "remember": Israel, remember your redemptive deliverance from Egypt; Christian, remember your redemptive deliverance at the Cross. "Do this in remembrance of me" is an exhortation for dynamic recall. "Memory . . . must be a meaningful memory" ("A Christian Perspective for the Teaching of History" by George Marsden, in *A Christian View of History?* George Marsden and Frank Roberts, eds., 34).

HISTORY INDISPENSABLE TO THEOLOGY

Why did God reveal Himself historically? We may note a theological value of this concept.

The Bible is more than enchanting stories, exalted poetry, and divine counsel. It is a high-powered record of a regenerating God entering the arena of human history in order to glorify Himself before our faces, that we who were made in His image might come to understand what that really means. Who can measure the mysterious wonder of the plaintive question: "Adam, where art thou?"

An overpowering lesson at this point is the intimate relationship which exists between eternity and time. "The Word was made flesh." "God has spoken in His Son." The Eternal stooped down. The Rich became poor. Indeed, all history is to be viewed in the light of this powerful humiliation: from creation to final judgment, from new birth to new earth. Paul Jewett says of Gen. 3:15, "and what is this protevangelium but the promise that God will not cease to act in history until he has destroyed man's moral foe . . . ?" (Quoted by I. E. Amaya, ETS, v. 14, pt. 2, Spring 1971, 69).

To devalue the historical parts of Scripture is to mar the magnificent glory of this continuous stooping. As the eternal and the human belong to Jesus Christ, so revealed truth and history belong together. "Remove history, and there is no truth . . . ; obscure the revelation and there is only history, subject

to human interpretation" ("History and Truth: A Study of the
Axiom of Lessing," by G. W. Romiley, in *The Evangelical
Quarterly*, v. 18, 1946, 196).

God, though eternal and transcendent, holy and thus separate from His created universe—needing nothing He has
made—though dwelling in light unapproachable and in His
perfections inexpressible, is as comfortable on earth with us
as He is in heaven. A historical Bible affirms the congeniality
of time and eternity; yet the history of the church at certain
points reflects a consistent inability to receive this. How can
harmony exist, it has been asked, between the eternal and
temporal, the spiritual and physical, the divine and human,
God and man? Must not one or the other suffer loss?

These questions bring to mind the numerous philosophies
and theologies in and out of the Christian Church which have
wittingly or unwittingly sought to deny or devalue the God-
man, Christ Jesus: Platonism, Gnosticism, Ebionism, Subor-
dinationism,   Arianism,   Pelagianism,   Nestorianism,
Eutychianism, Monotheletism, Monophysitism, Rationalism,
Deism, Unitarianism, and Socinianism, to name a few. These
all deny in one way or another that the Word, as defined in
Scripture, became flesh, as likewise defined.

To say that God gave His revelation through the medium
of human history means that the spiritual and the physical are
mutually consonant. They belong! To deny this is to violate
pure wisdom and to invalidate the triumph of grace. God created
the heavens, and He also created the earth and the sea, and
all that is in them. He called to sin-scarred Adam and Eve and
said, "Hey, I want to talk to you." Later He chose a lowly
insignificant stiff-necked tribes-people . . . a humble shepherd
boy . . . a stammering prophet. He entered our ken, now with
imperceptible voice and then with irresistible arm, to demolish
the ramparts of evil and to introduce incalculable order to
incalculable disorder.

Though the Church has struggled through the centuries
to understand this spiritual-physical tension, its magnificent

creeds yet bear eloquent testimony to the truth of our text: God has spoken and acted in the events of human history. Eternal truth *can* be made known through physical instrumentalities.

Some years ago, I discovered in a library a thin, old, dusty unused book simply entitled Monophysitism. The title and the book's condition held little promise. The author proved me wrong. With philosophical and theological argument, he pointed out the flaws of this ancient christological error and in a masterful statement underscored our point: "The incarnation brought divine and human together. Resurrection fixed this union. The ascension gave humanity an eternal place among eternal things" (*Monophysitism*, A. A. Luce, SPCK, 1920, p. 135).

HISTORY INDISPENSABLE TO FAITH

Our Christian faith is absolutely dependent upon the recorded events of Scripture; without this redemptive history, faith would be emptied of evidence. Hebrews 11:6 says that faith requires a God who acts. Carl Henry has written, "The promotion of faith is always within the framework of historical fact" (*God, Revelation, and Authority*, v. 2, ch. 22, p. 321).

In 1 Corinthians 15, Paul says the gospel concerns Jesus crucified, buried, and risen. He goes on to say that faith in this gospel cannot be indifferent to these well-corroborated events. Romans 10:9 calls on us to confess the Lord Jesus and believe that God has raised Him from the dead in order to be saved. The apostle uses a factual event and gives it a theological interpretation. "If Christ has not been raised . . . your faith is vain" (1 Corinthians 15:14; Marshall: *Luke, Historian and Theologian*, p. 46). The Bible writers under God's superintendence wrote history, but not mere history. As surely as they were narrating actual events, they were disclosing matters of universal redemptive significance.

In Romans 15:4 we are told "whatsoever things were written aforetime were written for our learning, that we through patience and comfort of the Scriptures might have hope." From our vantage point today, what then may we learn from these foregoing thoughts?

1. God, though mysterious and awesome in nature, is historically alive; it is His nature to declare by word and act. "I am God and there is none like Me, declaring things . . . ." In John 1:18, the only-begotten Son is "declaring the Father." God is always in the declarative mode.

2. Having set out on this declarative track, He must explain Himself. He must give meaning to His word-act in order to give understanding. Historical narrative without interpretation is insecure and vulnerable to those who would pervert its message. God is always in the interpretive mode.

This revealed meaning is found to be redemptive, gracious, and hopeful, in the believing consequence of which sinners are made to sit in heavenly places. God is always in the restorative mode. He declares in order that we may hear. He explains in order that we may understand what we've heard. He restores in order that we may obey what we've understood. We have referred to Luke several times. Have we referred to a historian or a theologian? I. Howard Marshall put it this way: "Because he was a theologian, he had to be a historian. His view of theology led him to write history" (Marshall, 52).

There are lessons for us in the comic pages. In the syndicated cartoon strip "Shoe," we observe little Skyler at his schoolroom desk, eager but inept, and thoroughly befuddled with the teachers's question. "Skyler, quick, what's nine times seven?" He reaches: "Oh, high 50s, low 60s, somewhere in there?" "No," glares the teacher. Skyler head in his hands, replies to no one in particular, "That's what I hate about math; no gray areas."

Perhaps just the opposite is true for most of us. Too many gray areas; too little of the precision that math offers. Too many choices to make. Too many fears, struggles, difficult relationships—and, like Skyler, we get confused. In the opening words of Alvin Toffler's The Third Wave, *he captures the feeling: "We live in a time when terrorists play death games with hostages, as currencies careen amid rumors of a third world war, and as embassies flame and storm troopers in many lands lace up their boots. We stare in horror at the headlines, 'Banks tremble, governments of the world are reduced to paralysis or imbecility.' Faced with all of this, a massed chorus of cassandras fill the air with doom songs. The proverbial man in the street says the world has gone mad while the expert points to all the trends leading toward catastrophe."*

In these chapters we have been hearing words like truth, light, power, seed, and food used to describe the Bible. Yet, there is more. We live and serve in a tough world, more difficult than many of us can handle and which none can handle alone. **Dr. Wayne E. Colwell,** *professor of Psychology at Western Seminary, guides us to understand that even in this kind of world we can turn to the gracious, healing, reviving, restoring Word of God. He presents the Word as our Counselor.*

THE WORD AS COUNSELOR:
Its Psychological Dimension

WAYNE E. COLWELL

THY servant meditates on Thy
statutes.
Thy testimonies are my
delight, my counselors.
(Psalm 119:23b-24)

An incident took place this summer that provides the object lesson for the message to follow. A colleague told me he had a Bing cherry tree on his property, that his family had picked all it wanted, and I would be welcome to pick what was left. Delighted, I said yes and asked for more details. It turned out there was a slight prerequisite. This was a tall tree, and my colleague had a short ladder. To reach the cherries I would need a ladder longer than his, because he had picked everything within reach. Fortunately, I own an eight foot aluminum stepladder, which happened to be two feet taller than my colleague's.

Overall the experience was enjoyable, reminiscent of the last time I had picked cherries—when I was eleven years old.

It came back to me, for instance, after I had dropped my bucket, to use a wire hook to hang the pail on a limb. This is like having three hands.

But that cherry tree was located on the side of a hill. Now it is quite possible to go two or three steps up a ladder without worrying how it is placed, but if you are going up near the top, great care must be taken. I not only had difficulty finding a level spot, but also discovered that if one leg sinks deeply into soft soil while the other three legs of the ladder hold firm, trouble awaits on the third or fourth step.

STEPLADDER THEOLOGY

God gave me some spiritual lessons that day with the stepladder that I trust will be useful to you. I use the stepladder as an analogy for one's life.

1. The ladder needs to be set on solid ground—straight and level, stable, no holes. The higher you climb, the more important a solid foundation becomes.

2. Ultimate usefulness of the ladder depends on successfully mounting it a step at a time.

3. The most work is usually done from the middle of the ladder, but sometimes you work from the top.

4. Each of the four legs of the stepladder represents an aspect of living that is necessary for spiritual and psychological health. If one leg is damaged or missing there will be instability. If in your mind's eye you can picture a stepladder, label the legs—relationships (view of others); self-concept (view of self); capabilities (knowledge and skills); and commitment (responsiveness).

5. The steps of the ladder represent stages of growth in one's character. These are identified in 2 Peter 1:5-7 as: moral excellence, knowledge (prudence), self-control, perseverance, godliness, brotherly kindness, and love.

Let's relate these to the theme verse of Western Seminary's

sixtieth anniversary: "Forever, O Lord, Thy Word is settled in heaven" (Psalm 119:89). As I spoke of a stepladder needing a dependable foundation, what could be more certain than this picture of the Word of God resting on a foundation laid in heaven? This Word, itself, is like a building rising from a strong foundation. It will stand when all else fails. In this era of instant everything—ready-to-serve, ready-to-eat food, microwave ovens, and drive-in restaurants—some of us have even developed fast prayers for fast foods. There is the consummate hazard of sermonettes producing Christianettes. There is the temptation to follow the laws of expediency and moral relativism instead of returning to the Bible as our reference point.

Sailors of old, I am told, believed it dangerous to navigate by close-at-hand reference points such as islands, mountain peaks, or passing ships. They looked to the stars. Let us look to the Word forever settled in heaven. We need this kind of bearing in order not to be tossed to and fro by waves and every wind of doctrine, the trickery and craftiness of deceitful men (Ephesians 4:14).

The Scriptures offer us God's power. The Gospel of Christ is the power of God unto salvation. "The Word of God is living and active and sharper than any two-edged sword, piercing as far as the division of soul and spirit, joints and marrow, and able to judge the thoughts and intentions of the heart" (Hebrews 4:12). This book reveals a Person powerful enough to give us spiritual life, and principles that guide and direct us to live the Christian life effectively.

NAGGING PROBLEMS OF LIFE

In contrast to a sure Word and a complete revelation of God's power, let us consider some of the problems of man. As Isaiah said when he saw the Lord, "Woe is me, for I am ruined, because I am a man of unclean lips" (Isaiah 6:5). People have problems and, like Isaiah, the problems look darkest in the presence of a holy God. I have made a list of problems that have been presented to me in the counseling office. As I name these problems may I suggest that you see if you can relate to them. Perhaps you have faced these same dilemmas or know someone who has.

First are some fears. Afraid to leave the house, cross a bridge, appear in public, be alone. Fearful of spouse leaving, of being battered, of being criticized, of being intimate. Fear of mistakes being repeated, thus suspicion and mistrust of one's mate.

Next are some life struggles that cause people to question God's presence in their lives: unable to find God's will vocationally; unable to get a church immediately on graduating from seminary; unable to control an appetite, resulting in addictive behavior such as bulimia, alcoholism, prescription drug abuse, etcetera; unable to sense God working all things together for good: in losses of health, income, mate, parent, and inheritance; or in indebtedness, injury, or destructive family upbringing.

Then there are people in conflict with authority. Instead of cooperation there is antagonism, and instead of humor and obedience, resentment and rebellion. Conflict results in children distancing themselves from parents, in job loss, in divorce, in violence, in abuse, and so on.

Another set of issues arises over self-concept: low self-esteem, perfectionism, guilt, and inferiority feelings. The results include social withdrawal, depression, hypersensitivity to evaluation and more.

Yet another group of problems may be classified as direct and indirect expressions of hostility. Of these, the indirect expressions are really the more insidious because in these we tend to injure ourselves as well as others—procrastination, being late, overeating, blaming, displacing (that is, suppressing anger toward a boss or spouse and becoming overly angry with one's children instead), complaining, being contentious, and so on.

Finally, there are problems due to people challenging God's Word on such things as the roles of wife and husband, sexuality, or divorce. Others complain or feel pain when the husband or wife does not measure up to biblical standards.

These are obviously serious problems, but please note also that it is not a list of heinous crimes. They are nagging problems that probably beset a substantial number of us.

Although the list is not exhaustive, it is somewhat illustrative of the human condition and lets us know that all is not well, even in the personal lives of evangelical Christians, from which this sample of problems is taken.

THE LADDER FIRMLY SET

Having acknowledged man's problems, it is important now to consider God's provision. Recall Isaiah's commission: After he saw himself in relation to a holy God and cried out "Woe is me!" one of the seraphim "touched his mouth with a burning coal, saying, 'Behold, this has touched your lips; and your iniquity is taken away, and your sin is forgiven' " (Isaiah 6:5-7).

Isaiah's work was first founded on God's cleansing. God gave him a new foundation, new stability, new power. Just as God's Word is forever founded in heaven, salvation becomes the foundation of our Christian life. "For no man can lay a foundation other than the one which is laid, which is Jesus Christ" (1 Corinthians 3:11). The Holy Spirit invites us through His Word to build upon this foundation with "gold, silver, and precious stones."

The hymn *Standing on the Promises* reminds us of the sure foundation on which we stand: "Standing on the promises that cannot fail, When the howling storms of doubt and fear assail, By the living Word of God I shall prevail, Standing on the promises of God."

According to 2 Peter 1:4, God "has granted His precious and magnificent promises in order that by them you might become partakers of the divine nature, having escaped the corruption that is in the world by lust."

It is on these promises that the Holy Spirit invites you to place the stepladder of your life. Make sure each leg referred to earlier is on solid footing.

The leg of relationship will find full endorsement in the Word as fellowship: fellowship with other believers, and with the Father and His Son Jesus Christ (1 John 1:3). The leg of self-concept will be enhanced by believing that God esteems us greatly, that He loved us and gave Himself for us, and that He made us in His image (Genesis 1:27). Self-esteem or self-acceptance can be based squarely on God's acceptance of us in the Beloved (Ephesians 1:6).

The leg of performance is surely strengthened when the Holy Spirit enables us to render service. "He is able to do exceeding abundantly above all that we ask or think, according to the power that works in us" (Ephesians 3:20). "I can do all things through Him who strengthens me" (Philippians 4:13). Much of our identity comes from this leg of doing. Many of us use performance to overcompensate for poor relationship skills or low self-esteem. Placing more weight on this corner of the ladder may make us dangerously unstable. A single well-placed criticism can send us toppling if our identities are based solely on performance. Remember that we are more than what we do.

The fourth equally important leg on this metaphorical stepladder is commitment. God wants us to heed His Word. "But prove yourselves doers of the Word, and not merely hearers who delude themselves" (James 1:22). "Occupy, or do business, until I return," said the nobleman to his servants (Luke 19:13), a reference to Christ and His followers.

CLIMBING THE LADDER

Now with this living ladder placed firmly on the rock of our salvation, it is time to climb. Peter writes: Make every effort to add to your faith . . . (2 Peter 1:5 NIV). The NASB reads: "Applying all diligence in your faith . . . ."

To live a separated, sanctified life requires an exercised, spiritually-in-shape style of life. Disciplined effort is called for. It does not come overnight. It comes slowly like the gradual physical conditioning of a soldier or athlete.

Step one is moral excellence. "Thy Word is a lamp unto my feet and a light unto my path" (Psalm 119:105). God's principles imbedded in the Scriptures are there to help us with each step we take. After salvation comes that first step of moral excellence. Do not underestimate this. Many stumble here and never really get much further in their Christian growth. "How can a young man keep his way pure? By keeping it according to Thy Word (Psalm 119:9).

Step two is knowledge. Knowledge without morality is a dangerous thing. "Teach me good discernment and knowledge, for I believe in Thy Commandments" (Psalm 119:66).

Knowledge applied to life situations, or wisdom, is described as "first pure, then peaceable, gentle, reasonable, full of mercy and good fruits, unwavering, without hypocricy" (James 3:17).

Step three is self-control. Matthew Henry defines self-control as moderation in desiring and using the good things of life. Materialism is inconsistent with an earnest desire after God and Christ. Another view would be that of impulse control. Suppose you had the impulse while studying to eat a dish of ice cream. If you are drawn to the refrigerator as if by a magnet, you lack impulse control. Next time try asking yourself, "What responsibility am I avoiding?"

You may still eat a dish of ice cream, but now it will be by choice. Perhaps you will prepare a smaller serving or pour a cup of tea instead, or simply continue studying. Choosing gives you one chance to control your impulses. Otherwise you are simply being led along rather than exercising self-control.

Step four is perserverance. The Greek word transliterated "that which remains under" is a picture of the silver-smelting process in which precious metal heated by fire melts to the bottom with the dross burning off at the top. Perseverance, or endurance, is what produces maturity in our lives. "And let endurance have its perfect result, that you may be perfect and complete, lacking in nothing" (James 1:4).

Step five is godliness. Building on the preceding character traits of moral excellence, self-control, and perseverance, acquisition of knowledge about God will certainly produce personal piety, an awareness of God in one's life. God's character is communicated to us in His written, living Word.

Step six is brotherly kindness revealed over and over as loving one another, a reciprocal love, true fellowship. "Bear one another's burdens, and thus fulfill the law of Christ" (Galatians 6:2).

Step seven is Christian (agape) love. This is the top rung in the progression. Agape is a type of love that seeks no reward. It is an unselfish giving for Christ's sake. "We know love by this, that He laid down His life for us; and we ought to lay down our lives for the brethren" (1 John 3:16). On this level it is especially important to examine our motives to be sure they are pure.

These steps mark the growth and development of Christians and, more pointedly, of Christian leaders. From our first days of knowing the Lord, our character is being formed for future ministry. It is especially important to be "adding to" our saving faith the several steps of sanctification: moral excellence, knowledge, and self-control. The next step defines entry into ministry, perseverance. God often sees fit not to place a seminary graduate immediately into a pastorate or other Christian profession. Could it be that this serves His purpose of making certain that perseverance becomes a part of our character?

Do not hurry to get past the present phase of your development. It is here that you may experience depression, or extreme panic, or you may question temporarily God's call or even doubt God's existence, and want to "ride off into the sunset" or something equally counterproductive. God often tests our character, as an engineer might test an automobile, to see if we will be durable under stress.

When these first phases are successfully developed one is then ready for effective ministry, utilizing the top three steps on the ladder: godliness—an awareness of God in your life; brotherly kindness—reciprocal love and fellowship; and agape love—selfless giving for Christ's sake.

I submit to you that most of your service will come while standing solidly on the steps of perseverance and godliness. And when these are firmly established in your character you are indeed in a position for ministering to others: planting, watering, pruning, harvesting; or more literally, evangelizing, teaching, disciplining and discipling.

We have considered man's problems and God's provision for growth, viewing the steps in 2 Peter as a model for normal spiritual development. But what if someone slips on one of the steps or falls completely off the ladder? Let us look now at God's provision for healing.

GOD'S PROVISION FOR HEALING

In many cases the problems mentioned above that were brought to the counseling office could have been prevented by properly following God's program for Christian growth, by adding to one's faith the seven steps of sanctification. This is utilizing the Word as Counselor at a preventative level.

God is also in the business of remediation. "The Lord is compassionate and gracious, slow to anger and abounding in lovingkindness (Psalm 103:8). God cares when people are heartbroken. In Psalm 119, "whole heart" is mentioned five times (verses 2,10,34,69,145). "Heart" in God's Word is understood to encompass the intellect, the emotions, and the will. When we stumble or have a problem, it is well to remember that God cares how we think, and feel, and decide. Nowhere is this more apparent than in the Psalms.

The healing of comfort. Because problem-laden people often do not actively read the Bible, we are faced with the delicate task of speaking the truth in love, of comforting "those who are in any affliction with the comfort with which we ourselves are comforted by God" (2 Corinthians 1:4).

Comfort is a word that can guide us in our manner of ministering to others. Listen rather than lecture. "Be quick to hear, slow to speak" (James 1:19). Educate rather than evaluate. Pay careful attention to a person's need for acceptance. As Dr. Stan Ellisen puts it, "The Bible is a smorgasbord, but do not try to feed it to someone all at once." A little variety and light servings, please.

> Don't unload a truckload
> Not a peck of this, a can of that
> A bag of this, a bottle of that
> But a banquet.
> And sometimes just cookies and a glass of milk
>   will do.

The healing of acceptance. The challenge of helping someone with a problem when you have the solution is getting that person to see and adopt the solution. This takes more than telling, selling, or yelling. The essence of helping someone lies first in the relationship you develop with that person, not in the information you impart. Many people already have more information than they know what to do with. They lack an atmosphere of acceptance in which they can objectively sort out their dilemmas and incorporate the suggestions they have already been given.

When the occasion comes to give counsel, refer to God's Word. Properly shared, the Bible can buoy one's spirit. From a human standpoint, Psalm 119 is probably the "reflection of one, or more likely of many, minds on a long course of events belonging to the past, but preserved in memory; recollections arranged in such a way as not only to recall experiences of past days, but to supply religious support under similar trials" (Ellicott's Commentary, v. IV, 260).

"Religious support under similar trials"—how well this expresses the counseling value of Psalm 119 and many other parts of Scripture as well. Why is it so helpful? Because of the content which consists largely of praises of God's Word, exhortations to peruse it and use it, reverence for it, prayers for its proper influence, and complaints against the wicked who despise it.

Comfort others by counseling people to peruse and then use the Word of God while you promise to pray for its proper influence in their lives.

Doubtless we will find ourselves as believers needing both growth and healing. Better an ounce of prevention, but oh, how satisfying it is to experience a pound of cure. It usually hurts and it usually costs, but we thank God for His healing provision.

CONCLUSION

In summary let me remind you again of the Word as Counselor. Even though you may seek the counsel of others, be sure the direction you receive accords with God's Word. Like the ancient sailors, beware of close-at-hand reference points. Seek a heavenly, eternal perspective when you need guidance, and may we say with the psalmist, "Thy servant meditates on Thy statutes. Thy testimonies are my delight, my counselors" (Psalm 119:23b-24).

During a recent gubernatorial election campaign in our state, one of the candidates answered the question of why he was seeking the office in a day when political life is so trying. "You have to have the fire in your bones," he asserted. I wondered at the time whether he realized the sort of company in which he was including himself, if he knew the true source of the metaphor he had chosen. It was a higher source, indeed. It was those unmatched men of God, the fearless, outspoken prophets of the Old Testament who testified of that "fire in the bones." They had the stark realization that they had heard from on high the very voice of God and with that realization they would face even death to declare it. The fire that burned in their bones should well burn in ours as well.

It is not enough to merely know the Word of God; consuming, compelling—we must know it and we must feel it. Herein lies the mystery of ministry, that a man or woman can be the very voice of God to a lost world because of the Word of God which is in our hands. But it is a word that cannot be spoken before it is heard. What a fearful thing to attempt to speak for God without ever knowing His Word. But equally fearful is to have His Word and His call to speak, and to remain silent.

Dr. Duane A. Dunham, *professor of New Testament Language and Exegesis at Western Seminary, directs us to consider the Word as God's prophetic call.*

THE WORD AS PROPHETIC SPOKESMAN:
Its Prophetic Call

DUANE A. DUNHAM

DIVINE Scripture is also human literature. It has all the earmarks or features of human literary productions—plots, puns, heroes and heroines, villains and cowards—all recorded without error. It has been analyzed, criticized, imitated by admirers, despised by enemies, wounded in the house of its friends, and yet it stands as the most unique literature in all of human history.

The Bible documents are unique because they come from God. They are described as the very utterances of the holy, eternal, transcendent, omnipotent God who speaks and reveals Himself to sinful, finite, transitory, and powerless humans.

THE WORD AS PROPHECY

At the center of the uniqueness of Scripture is prophecy. Alvin Toffler's popular book *Future Shock* hit our American bookstands in 1970 and immediately sold millions of copies.

Toffler looks into the future as a man who cannot predict what
WILL happen, but only what is likely or desirable. The book
is almost devoid of any reference to the institutional church or
the clergy and makes no place for the words of Scripture. This
is strikingly inconsistent. The Bible is the one ancient literary
source which not only is futurist in outlook, an attitude which
Toffler admires, but also stands as demonstrably accurate
beyond the possibilities of mere chance. Toffler's inconsistency
is explained by the fact that his envisioned future is a future
without God, predicated not upon revelation or prophecy, but
upon personal desires, shrewd analysis, and sheer guesswork—
plus the idealistic, unified hard work of concerned people.

The futures conceived by men have largely been dependent upon the brilliance and cooperation of mankind. But the
Scriptures' future is entirely the work of the omnipotent God.
Men's religions have come from cunning and occasionally in-
genious programs originated by brilliant men and promoted by
enthusiastic but deluded henchmen.

Other attempts at futurism, dating from the time of Plato's
Republic, have met with slight success. All pale into insignifi-
cance when compared to the prophetic Scriptures which give
so many and varied details about events which are now history,
but were future to the writers. It cannot be a fortuitous accident;
it is the plan and program of God.

The uniqueness of Bible prophecy almost guarantees its
misunderstanding, misinterpretation, and ridicule. Although
the prophetic Scriptures have held a fascination for the godly
expositors, they are often frustrated by interpretational difficulties. While con men are always sure of the details of tomorrow's
world (or the world of tomorrow!), Scripture does not make
it nearly so clear. The ridicule of the Bible is commonly fueled
by us frail humans, who, with the best of intentions go off
half-cocked, making our speculative ideas into authoritative
pronouncements—which with their too often erroneous views
may become the basis for fellowship. The result for such impul-

sive teachers is more than occasionally date-setting, which Jesus in no uncertain terms said is impossible. The result for listeners is a misguided fanaticism such as can be illustrated time and again in church history, or a settled skepticism of unbelief from which it is all but impossible to retrieve them.

The study of the Scriptures as prophecy could lead us into a labyrinth of intermingled sociological, theological, and historical data that would take years to unravel. For our purposes today, however, we shall limit our discussion to the question: What practical value is the prophetic element of Scripture?

THE NATURE OF BIBLICAL PROPHECY

Although biblical prophecy is unique, it is by no means unique in the sense that only the Judeo-Christian religions have prophecy. There seems to be a common thread among most if not all peoples of the earth that a god exists who makes himself known, but who speaks to especially chosen people. The Greeks had their Delphic oracle as well as the women of Pythia and Sybil who spoke and wrote the oracles of God. To the east, the Egyptians and Babylonians had the movement of the heavenly bodies and the consulting of viscera of animals by their priests (Ezekiel 21:21), to find God's guidance while other nations watched the movement of animals, the leaves of tress, etc.

Scripture's uniqueness is in both the content and the accuracy of the message. It is, in fact, from God, and therefore authoritative and inerrant in its declarations. The writer of Hebrews expresses this in his profoundly complex and simple opening statement: "In many parts and in many ways God spoke of old to the fathers by the prophets, and in the last of these days He has spoken by His Son." The magnificent fact declared is that God has spoken to man in His Son and in His Word.

Scriptural prophecy is twofold. It foretells the future and it tells forth the will of God for the present. Most biblical prophecy concerns the prophet speaking to his times, indicating the will of God for His people. A significant portion also was a revelation of future events. In either case, it is a manifestation of the revelation of God to men. We term this process "special revelation," in that it is able to be specifically interpreted, whereas general revelation's meanings are diffused.

God's will is not immediately apparent to all. The fall has veiled Him and clouded our minds. We need His special acts of revealing Himself through special people in order to understand His will. Even the pagans saw the necessity for the gods to speak in special ways and at special times to special people. To describe the special people through whom God spoke, the Old Testament uses such terms as "seer" and "prophet" (1 Samuel 9:9).

To protect against the abuse of the prophetic gift or office, Deuteronomy 18:20-22 and Deuteronomy 13:1-5 give the methods of detection the children of Israel are to use in ascertaining a true and a false prophet. So important does God see the accurate delivery of His message that He declares false prophecy to be a capital offense (Deuteronomy 13:5), along with such other sins as witchcraft, blasphemy, rape, and murder.

Although the Lord Jesus indicates that John the Baptist was the greatest of the prophets, it is He Himself who is the chief prophet in the New Testament. It is He who reveals the Father to men both in unmistakable words and miraculous deeds. During His earthly ministry He condemned the inadequate expression of the leading religious men, vividly pointing to their hypocrisy.

After His ascension, the apostles take up the prophetic burden. The words and works of Jesus continue as the focal point of their teaching and preaching as they speak of God's will for the present and occasionally break into foretelling future events. Jesus is revealed and reveals the future in the last book of the New Testament, "The Revelation of Jesus Christ."

Similar to the Old Testament, the New Testament has both writing and nonwriting prophets; the former are the most prominent. The language and literary genres may differ, but the prophetic gift is still exercised in displaying the will and program of God. The writer of Hebrews expresses the superiority of New Testament revelation to the Old Testament by indicating the superiority of the Revelator, the Son of God. It is to this superior revelation, this prophetic word, that we give our attention and allegiance.

What we have in prophecy is God's message to us, without which we cannot either please or approach God. It is by His own grace that we have it, and by His grace we are enabled to understand and act in obedience to it.

INTERPRETATION OF BIBLE PROPHECY

While the prophet still lived, his prophecy was not always fully understood. Daniel 8:15, 1 Peter 1:10-12, and Revelation 7:13f. indicate that even after seeing the prophetic vision, the prophets sometimes did not understand the significance of everything they had seen. How much more difficult the interpretative task is for us who are separated from the prophets by time, culture, and language.

Interpreting prophecy has long been a battleground for the various millennial viewpoints. There is an especially crucial debate between the so-called amillennialists and premillennialists. When amillennialists approach unfulfilled prophecy, they have no qualms about changing their hermeneutics from the consistent historical grammatical platform from which all the precious doctrines of the reformed faith were launched. As premillennialists, we object to such change and insist on preserving the consistent, literal hermeneutic which leads to an admittedly simpler eschatology.

It might be fairly asked, why insist on a literal hermeneutic? Does this not make us rigid "letteristic" fundamentalists, parodied and pilloried in speech and essay? Of course, the question is addressed, not on the basis of some real or imagined guilt by association, but whether or not it is a valid hermeneutic. Simply put, literal interpretation aims to understand what the original writer intended his original readers to understand. We take these words in their most usual, ordinary, everyday meaning. This is not to say we then despise or refuse to allow figures of speech. Figures are as common in modern everyday speech as they are in a literary work such as Isaiah or John's gospel. Taken in context, they are easily understood. But this is a far cry from allegorism, the bane of sound exegetical sense from the earliest days. Citing this tendency carried to great lengths, Berkley Mickelson rightly observes about the allegorical methodology of the brilliant Philo: "As an exegete . . . Philo is an example of what not to do."

O. T. Allis in his *Prophecy and the Church* attacks the Scofield Bible and the dispensational theology it espouses. He rejects the principle of literal interpretation of prophecy for three reasons which do not address the question adequately. His reasons are: (1) "The Bible often contains figures of speech"; (2) since God is a Spirit, the most precious teachings of the Bible are spiritual; "these spiritual . . . realities are often set forth under the form of earthly objects"; (3) "the fact that the Old Testament is both preliminary and preparatory to the New Testament is too obvious to require proof."

He then argues from this last statement that the New Testament gives "a deeper and far more wonderful meaning" to the Old Testament passages than if they were strictly limited to their Old Testament contexts" (pp. 17-18). We certainly agree with these assertions. Dispensational premillennialism does not contradict them. But, by what principle or principles does reformed amillennialism decide when to apply these facts and thus end up with their millennial position? Much of their error derives from the oft-quoted statement: "Scripture is to be interpreted literally unless forbidden by context or theology." If a passage literally interpreted does not match theology, it becomes a type or allegory of some kind. Hence, Israel is the church without any New Testament writer stating it, and one thousand years is "a long period of time, a great epoch in human history" (Swete, *Commentary on Revelation,* p. 260). The amillennialist views Satan as currently bound in some spiritual way by the gospel, with no satisfactory explanation for his present powerful influence, for the reason given for his binding, nor of the warning by Peter of his current activities (1 Peter 5:8)! Likewise, the kingdom of Christ on earth is seen as a spiritual present kingdom, not a future, literal, physical one. We dispute all these on the basis of consistent hermeneutics.

THE NEED FOR CONSISTENT HERMENEUTICS

We may offer several basic defenses for a literal interpretation of prophecy. (1) If a literal interpretation is valid in passages dealing with soteriology and bibliology, what is there inherent in eschatology which requires a different hermeneutic? Reformed theology makes assertions about context, grammar, etcetera, then denies them when confronted with an eschatological passage. As an example of this, Geldenhuys in his New International Commentary on Luke says regarding 1:33, "Where hereafter mention is made of the eternal kingdom of Christ it is obvious that it is not the earthly 'house of Jacob' that is meant here, but His people in a spiritual sense." We ask, where is the contextual requirement for such a view? Where is the indication of a figure of speech or an underlying "spiritual" meaning?

(2) If fulfilled prophecies are perceived as literally fulfilled, does this not set a precedent for those not yet fulfilled? Consider the birthplace of Messiah, the destruction of Nineveh

and Tyre, the captivity of Israel, etcetera. All were predicted in the same style, and often in the same passages as eschatological truth. They were all literally fulfilled.

(3) Since the intent of prophecy is to be understood by those thus informed, what limits and guidelines are to be set on so-called spiritual interpretations? All too often only the limits of the expositor's imagination will check him. We can applaud Hodge's first rule of interpretation: "The words of Scripture are to be taken in their plain literal historical sense. That is, they must be taken in the sense attached to them in the age and by the people to whom they were addressed" (Charles Hodge, *Systematic Theology*, I:187). When dealing with prophecy Hodge asserts: "The literal interpretation of the Old Testament prophecies relating to the restoration of Israel and the future kingdom of Christ, cannot by possibility be carried out" (III:809). It is clear that his objections to a literal interpretation of the relevant passages are not dependent on the language, on supposed figures of speech, or on a change in the aura of the passage. It is based upon his theological objections to rebuilding the Temple, offering sacrifices, and placing Israel at the forefront of God's program once again. There are obviously some difficulties (i.e., the blood sacrifices being offered after the death of Christ) but to say that they are impossible and demand another interpretation is simply too facile a solution.

The plain literal nature of much of prophecy leads to a clear premillennialism. Even the figures of speech do not refute this, but on the contrary they enhance the doctrine. Much of prophecy, it is true, cannot be precisely determined (e.g., the meaning of the number of the beast); yet that should not be a license for spiritualizing a plain meaning.

PRACTICAL BENEFITS OF BIBLE PROPHECY

Without question, prophecy produces many results in daily lives, but I wish to emphasize the two which are most apparent and practical. But first I must issue a disclaimer: Prophecy does not tell us God's timetable. It does not allow the setting of dates, or the designating of current events as "prophecies fulfilled." It is not a preview of tomorrow's newspaper headlines. Many are the sensational sermons purporting to show "America's Place in Prophecy," "The Antichrist Today," etcetera. We do not deny that specific prophecies will be specifically fulfilled. However, a neglect of the wider context too often results in the error of naming tribulation prophecies as church-age happenings.

The Foremost Benefit of Hope. Perhaps the primary result is the Christian virtue of hope. Paul tells us hope is one of the three prime Christian virtues, along with faith and love. Some have decided that his meaning for the 1 Corinthians passage was that only love was worth developing and emphasizing. Nothing could be further from the truth! Each of these virtues is superior in its own way as properly used. The context of 1 Corinthians 13 is the recognition and employment of spiritual gifts; hence love, regard for the brethren, is of prime import here. When the scene changes to a consideration of Bible doctrine and theology, faith is superior. You are not saved by love, but by faith. You do not recognize the truth by love, but by faith.

Hope is the word of the future. Webster defines it: "confident trust in a future event; to desire with expectation of fulfillment." Hope is superior when motivation and endurance is in view. Romans 8:24-25 indicates this. Hope is an emotional and intellectual response to Scripture, specifically to prophecy. "For whatever was before written was written for our instruction, so that through endurance and the encouragement of the Scriptures we might have hope" (Romans 15:4).

Hebrews 6:9-20 needs a longer exposition than can be given here, but being built upon the exhortation and warning of verses 1-8, it proclaims a mighty climax to God's redeeming acts.

Hope is (1) an innoculation against spiritual sluggishness, which caused difficulty in their assembly (Hebrews 5:11-14 and 6:9-12). Hope is a motivator to spiritual growth.

Hope is (2) to be seized (6:13-18), being built on the promises of God. Note how covenant and promise are intimately intertwined with prophecy, and this results in hope—assured trust that God will honor His Word. God spoke in prophecy to Abraham, affirming His covenant both by His Divine Person and His authoritative Word. Is there a promise, a covenant, that is not prophetic at some point?

Our hope in Christ's fulfillment of all the promises is not something passive, not a spiritual gift; not something God does for us, but something we must grasp. In 6:18 we have a strong exhortation to seize the hope placed before us. The term rendered "seize" is *kratew* which has the idea of rule or conquer, "win and keep, especially by force" (Lidell Scott, p. 991). It is a strong term emphasizing personal action.

Hope is (3) not in vain, but as certain as the resurrection, ascension, and present session of Christ can make it (6:19-20). The figure of the anchor being in the harbor reflects the practice of the ancient sailing ships. When the crew could not enter a difficult harbor without jeopardizing the vessel, they would engage a smaller boat to take their anchor into the safe harbor and set it firmly. The larger ship would then winch its way into safety. Christ our anchor, already safely in the harbor, is surely drawing us to Himself. That is our hope.

Prophecy Designed to Produce Holiness (2 Peter 3). Only the scoffers maintain there is no just end to life as we know it, as noted by Peter (3:1- 4). These were perhaps traveling teachers or even members of the assembly who taught this pernicious error. Either they rejected the record of Christ's promise to return or they suggested that due to the passing of time His words were misinterpreted. Such belief will result in the total end of Christian hope, and issue in antinomian excesses as described in 2 Peter 2.

Rather, Peter teaches that the end of this age is as sure as the creation and the flood of Noah's day. This is decreed by the same Word as that which decreed creation and the flood (3:7).

God operates in a different time frame than we understand (3:8-9). It is not appropriate to think less of God's program or His decree to carry it out just because of the passing of time. God is event-centered, not time-centered in carrying out His will and plan.

Peter declares that the end of the age, the dissolving of the elements, and the discovery of all works makes a great and significant demand on us (3:10-13). Therefore, we must ask where our hope is founded: on personal abilities, family connections, worldly success? Or on Christ? Where must our time be invested? Making money, spending money, raising children, building houses, or gaining knowledge?

No one of these securities is evil in itself, and many are admirable, but we need to ask again: For what reason has God called us out of darkness into His marvelous light? Jesus emphasized the need to lay up in store heavenly treasures where no thief, moth nor rust can destroy them. Only spiritual things will remain forever. That person is a fool who calls himself a Christian, yet is more concerned with temporal things than with his relationship with God.

One of the Puritans reminds us, "Of what use is a golden cup if there is poison in it? What value is a silk stocking on a broken leg?" He then exhorts, "Do not be as men rowing a boat. They look one way and row another. Do not look towards heaven and row towards hell."

If one's Christian faith, knowledge of Scripture, or devotion to ministry does not result in holiness that permeates one's entire existence, his or her life is a failure. All the competence, charm, charisma and intellectual acumen one might possess cannot compensate for a filthy, unspiritual, unholy life. Today is the day to draw near to God, to weep over sin, and to plead for His victory in living a life of holiness. His prophetic Word calls us to a life of hope and holiness as we await His return.

Chapter by chapter, we have been celebrating the Word of God, and now we come to the final challenge. This is certainly not the final word on this subject, but it is our benediction. We sought to consider the many magnificent facets of the Scriptures, and have felt our minds and hearts overwhelmed by the reality of knowing our God as the God Who has spoken.

I have had on my bookshelf for several years two volumes which have helped me in my understanding of God. One is titled, The God Who Is There, *and the other,* The God Who Has Spoken. *I recently acquired a new volume which completes the set, as it were. It is titled,* The God Who Hears. *These three titles portray the great God whom we know and serve. He is a God who is not silent: He has spoken—and He listens. One of the glorious features of the Bible is its personal invitation into intimate communication with Him. That Divine-human adventure in the Bible brings us to the subject of effective prayer.*

*It is fitting that this benedictory chapter come from **Dr. Ralph H. Alexander,** professor of Hebrew Scripture at Western Seminary. By word and deed, he has consistently called attention to this privilege and challenge of prayer, a call that has earned the respect and response of fellow professors and students alike. He presents here a final facet of the Scriptures, the Word as prayer.*

THE WORD AS PRAYER:
Its Benediction

RALPH H. ALEXANDER

PROVERBS 28:9 declares: "If anyone turns a deaf ear to the law, even his prayers are detestable." This ancient proverb declares an essential principle on prayer. If we allow it to penetrate our thinking, it could radically affect our prayer life.

As I evaluate my own prayers and listen to those of others, I am convinced that the Word of God often has little influence upon our prayers. Perhaps the greatest influence comes from the many exhortations in the Scripture to pray. But even so we respond less frequently than we should.

What effect does the Word of God have upon the way I pray and the content of my prayers? Philippians 4:6 states that we should present our requests to God in everything. That we normally do. But often that is the extent of the Scripture's bearing upon my prayer life. Let us examine what a man of God in Scripture tells us about the effect of God's Word upon his prayers.

Daniel was a man of prayer. He was so consistent in his prayer life that his accusers knew with certainty that they could trap him if they could only manage to get the king to make a decree forbidding prayer to anyone except the king. Daniel allowed the Word of God to affect the content and the manner in which he prayed. His prayer recorded in chapter 9 is instructive in this respect. We shall examine that prayer—not as a model prayer, but as a model for instruction on how the Word of God should influence the way we pray.

PRAYER IN LIGHT OF GOD'S WORD

We read in Daniel 9:1-3: "In the first year of Darius son of Xerxes (a Mede by descent), who was made ruler over the Babylonian kingdom—in the first year of his reign, I, Daniel understood from the Scriptures, according to the word of the Lord given to Jeremiah the prophet, that the desolation of Jerusalem would last seventy years. So I turned to the Lord God and pleaded with him in prayer and petition, in fasting, and in sackcloth and ashes."

The first principle we learn from Daniel is that we should pray in light of the Word of God and about the Word as we read. Daniel had been studying the book of Jeremiah. In chapter 25 he read that the captivity of the Israelites was to last only seventy years. Reflecting upon the fact that those seventy years were almost complete, Daniel immediately began to pray to the Lord about the truth he had just been reading. This is the effect that the Word of God should have on all believers. As we read the Scriptures, what we read should cause us to talk to the Lord about it—whether we have been convicted, challenged, exhorted, instructed, or encouraged. This could, and should, change our whole approach to the reading and study of the Scripture. As we read, we should pray about what we read. Understanding the truth, we should lay hold of it and immediately discuss that truth and its application with our heavenly Father. This, in turn, encourages us to place confidence and faith in God's revelation and in His faithfulness to it.

Praying with Humility

Daniel's prayer shows us a second principle: The Word of God causes an attitude of humility and seriousness in prayer. Fasting, sackcloth, and ashes each have their root significance in the concept of humility (frequently accompanied by mourning and repentance). When one fasted, put on sackcloth and covered himself with ashes, he humbled himself before God with all seriousness.

Understanding the impact of the prophecy of Jeremiah, Daniel humbled himself before God and prayed with all seriousness. Prayer is no place for flippancy and arrogance. Yet how often do we insensitively tack on prayer to the beginning or end of a meeting as a formality? Or perhaps we respond as did a former colleague of mine when he and his wife decided to begin a time of devotions before retiring for the evening. First they read a portion of Scripture. Then my friend began their time of prayer by saying, "Dear Father, we thank you for this food . . ." He was going through the motions without really thinking about what he was doing. How often we do the same.

The words of 2 Chronicles 7:14 are not a promise for us, but this verse does reflect the proper attitude we should have when we come to pray: "If my people who are called by my name humble themselves, and pray and seek my face, and turn from their wicked ways, then I will hear from heaven, and will forgive their sin and heal their land." That is the attitude with which we ought to enter into prayer. Time in the Word of God encourages a genuine attitude of humility and seriousness when we pray.

Prayer Involves Confession

Beginning with verse 4, Daniel demonstrates that the Word of God has provided a foundation to prepare us for supplication. This preparation occurs through confession. Daniel's preparation through confession covers verses 4 through 15 while only four verses are alloted to his petition (16-19). As we will observe, that proportion underscores a significant factor in the way one ought to pray.

Daniel beautifully unfolds the twofold nature of confession. Confession of sin (with which we are most familiar) enables one to restore a proper relationship with God, providing true freedom in the relationship with our Lord. When a husband and wife have an argument, confession on the part of the offender enables the relationship to be restored and freedom to exist once again between them. So it is in our relationship with God.

The second aspect of confession is perhaps more foreign to us—especially in prayer: confession of who God is and what He does. This is the correct definition of praise. The English words "confess" and "praise" are translations of Hebrew words that come from the same root. As we understand the confession of sin to be the acknowledgment and declaration of sin, so praise is the acknowledgment and declaration of who God is and what He does. As Daniel prepares himself for petition, he confesses both the sin of Israel and the character and work of God. In fact, as Daniel praises (or confesses) God's character and works, the confession of sin is more clearly highlighted against the backdrop of God's person and works.

Daniel begins his confession with the praise of God as the master, one who is great, awe-inspiring, faithful, and loving. Therefore He is faithful to His revelation in the Mosaic covenant and loves to grant its blessings to those who are obedient (cf. Deuteronomy 7:12 and 10:17).

Reflecting upon this greatness, faithfulness, and love of God, Daniel immediately observed the antithesis in Israel's sin. The Israelites, in contrast to God's demonstrable character in verse 4, have been disobedient servants (verses 5-6). They have failed to follow God's standard revealed in the Mosaic covenant. They have perverted the truth and actively perpetrated their wickedness. This led them to bold and audacious acts of rebellion against God, continually turning aside from God's Word. They became so callous to God's Word that they refused to listen to His warnings through His prophets.

Daniel recognized that Israel had no right to request God's favor unless they genuinely loved Him. Such love is demonstrable by knowing and doing the principles of God's Word (Deuteronomy 6:4-9). My son asks me to teach him how to swim. But when I tell him what he needs to do in order to learn to swim, he won't follow the instructions. He lacks confidence in them. By analogy that is what we often do in our prayers. We ask God to help us to witness, yet we never plan to go and talk with anyone. Or we ask God to teach us how to pray, but we do not want to take time to find out what He has told us about prayer in the Bible. It makes no sense to be asking God in prayer what we are unwilling to learn from His Word and to do.

In verses 7-8, Daniel declares that God is always righteous while Israel's shame and unfaithfulness demonstrate that she was wrong. Every time we meditate upon God's righteousness, we cannot help but be reminded of any sin that currently exists in our lives. We need to do this frequently.

PRAYER SEEKS GOD'S COMPASSION

Daniel continues his confession by proclaiming that God is compassionate and forgiving like a parent (verse 9) even though Israel, as a child, has been rebellious and disobedient to her heavenly Father (verse 10). Israel has not lived according to the principles of God's covenant revealed to Moses. Mankind normally responds to rebellion strongly and harshly; God has responded to Israel with compassion and forgiveness that is not deserved. The terms for "compassion" and "forgiveness" are intensive words emphasized by their plural forms. God's compassion and forgiveness are overwhelming. As a loving Father, His love for Israel has so involved Him emotionally that He yearns to forgive them of their rebellion so they can enjoy the good and productive life to which he has called them. The only hope of Israel is based on the truth of Psalm 130:3-4: "If you, O LORD, kept a record of sins, O LORD, who could stand? But with you there is forgiveness; therefore you are feared." This reflects the marvelous character of God expressed in Lamentations 3:22-23—"Because of the Lord's great love we are not consumed, for his compassions never fail. They are new every morning; great is your faithfulness."

PRAYER ALLOWS GOD'S DISCIPLINE

God's love for His people Israel and His faithfulness to His Word was demonstrated in His fatherly discipline of Israel in the Babylonian captivity (verse 11). Discipline has a twofold thrust: correction with its instruction, and prevention—to keep us from incorrect habit patterns. God's fatherly love has led Him to correct Israel's rebellion and unfaithfulness and to seek thereby to prevent her from continuing her previous addiction to rebellion. God equally loves each of us in the same manner today.

God said in the Mosaic covenant (Deuteronomy 29) that He would bring great disasters upon His people—even dispersion among the nations—if they turned from His ways. The Israelites in Daniel's day were experiencing the faithfulness of God to do what He had said (verse 12)—to discipline Israel through exile. We like God to be faithful to His promises until it concerns discipline. But He is always faithful to all of His Word. He is righteous (or right) in His chastisement as He is in all His works (verses 13-14). God's righteousness was vindicated by Israel's present disobedience (for they still had not obeyed Him) and stubborn refusal to turn from their iniquity or consider God's truth (verse 13). The fact that a people (or individual) is still experiencing discipline means that they have not yet confessed their sin and repented concerning it. Israel had not been very responsive to God's discipline. Are we?

Daniel concludes his confession of God's character and the sin of Israel by highlighting the immutability of God. When Israel, under Moses, finally came to the recognition and repentance of their sin, the Lord forgave Israel and showed His compassion by delivering her from Egypt. Likewise, if Israel will confess and repent of her sin now, God will also forgive her and demonstrate His compassion in delivering her from the Babylonian exile. God has not changed. For Israel it was a matter of transfer of learning. So it is for us today. Remembrance of God's past deeds (recorded in His Word) is important (as the psalmists frequently show us), for it causes us to be encouraged that our immutable God will be faithful to His Word today even as He has been in the past. If He worked then, so He works NOW!

PRAYER INVOLVES BOLD PETITIONS

Having prepared himself for supplication through confession of God's person and works (praise) and, by contrast, the sins of Israel, Daniel begins his petition. Daniel's requests are anticlimactic, for an answer was expected after confession. The stage had been set by Daniel's praise of God. If God possesses the character that Daniel has just recounted in verses 4-15, then the answers are fairly clear and expected.

Each request that Daniel will make will be based upon the character of God revealed in His Word (and confessed above) or in light of the Scripture he was reading (Jeremiah 25:11-12 and 29:10; 2 Chronicles 6:21). In like manner our petitions should not be arbitrary, random, self-centered, hurried requests. They should be based upon the attributes of God, His works, and His principles revealed in the Scripture. I do not pray boldly for a place to live, for my sick mother, or for my studies by simply giving it a little more "umph." I can pray boldly only on the basis of God's character and His Word as the foundation of each request.

Daniel implores God for each request. He commands God to answer. Initially this appears extremely audacious on Daniel's part. How can he (or anyone else) ever command God? But we must recognize that Daniel's bold entreaty was only possible because each request is based upon his understanding of God's Word and the person of God revealed therein. We too can pray boldly in the same manner, if we do so on the same basis.

Four requests are made by Daniel, each with its unique basis (verses 16-19). *First,* Daniel calls upon God to remove His wrath from Jerusalem (verse 16). The basis? God's righteousness—righteousness to forgive sins of the current generation as well as their forefathers. Righteousness to be faithful to His promise to restore Jerusalem, His chosen city (cf. Psalm 132). Righteousness to correct the poor testimony of the Israelites who presently were a reproach among the nations (cf. Jeremiah 33:4-9).

Second, Daniel implores God to listen favorably to his request that the Jerusalem temple no longer lie desolate (verse 17). Why? For the Lord's sake! After all, the psalmist tells us, "The Lord has chosen Zion, he has desired it for his dwelling: 'This is my resting place forever and ever; here I will sit enthroned, for I have desired it'" (Psalm 132:13-14). Daniel was more concerned about the Lord than about Israel or himself. The desolate sanctuary was a blight on God's name. In the ancient Near East nations believed that a country's god was weak if he could not defend his land and care for his people. As the nations looked upon the desolations in Judah and Jerusalem, they reproached the God of Israel as weak and incapable of caring for His people. Therefore, Daniel made his request "for the Lord's sake" so that His name would be vindicated among the nations. How often do we make our requests for "the Lord's sake?" Or is our concern more "for our own sake," for what people will think of us?

Third, Daniel commands God to hear and see how bad the destruction of Jerusalem was and the desolations of the

Israelites. And upon what basis is this request made? It was
made on the basis of God's compassion, certainly not on the
basis of Israel's righteousness (verse 18). This is a request for
grace. The Israelites don't deserve it. So often we think we
really deserve favors from God and get a little ticked off when
God does not perform as we wish. But we must remember that
we deserve nothing. That God would look and take pity on
the desolation of Jerusalem and the Israelites is strictly a manifestation of His great compassion for both. There is no other
basis upon which Daniel could have made this request. It
reflects humility on his part.

Fourth, the culminating request is intensive. With a series
of imperatives, Daniel calls upon God to hear, forgive, act,
and not delay! How can Daniel be so bold? Because he bases
this petition upon God's person (His sake) and upon the fact
that Jerusalem and the Israelites are called by His name (verse
19). We, as Christians, are also called by His name today. Are
we as concerned for God's reputation as was Daniel? Are we
busy making requests for our own sake so that we might look
good in others' eyes? We ought to be making petition in order
that God's name might be honored in this world.

PRAYER MOVES GOD TO FULFILL HIS WORD

God delights in those who pray according to His character
and His revelation. God began to answer Daniel's prayer before
he finished. In fact, God began to answer Daniel's requests
before he uttered them. Why? Because He knew that Daniel
would base his requests on God's attributes and Word. Therefore, God would answer with certainty—as He always does
when our petitions are based on His person and work. The
angel Gabriel was sent at the beginning of Daniel's supplication
and arrived with the answer before he finished that supplication
four verses later. This is not to say God will always answer
our prayer with the same speed, but we can know with certainty

that if we pray on the basis of God's character and Word, God will answer! In Daniel's case, the answer brought an understanding of the fulfillment of Jeremiah's prophecy.

The challenge from Daniel seems clear. The Word of God is foundational for any prayer. Each request we make should be based upon the Word of God and the person of God revealed therein. As we read and study the Word, it should cause us to pray about what we read. It should produce humility and seriousness in our prayers. It should create confidence, boldness, purpose, and expectation when we pray in light of the Scripture and on the basis of God's person and works.

Elijah was also a man who prayed in this manner. "Elijah was a man of like nature with ourselves, and he prayed fervently that it might not rain, and for three years and six months it did not rain on the earth" (James 5:17).

We too can pray with the same boldness and effectiveness as Daniel and Elijah. We can likewise expect answers from a God Who delights to answer according to His Word. "The prayer of the upright is God's delight" (Proverbs 15:8).